I'll Tell You No Lies

MCCRINA

I'LL TELL YOU NO LIES

FARRAR STRAUS GIROUX
NEW YORK

Farrar Straus Giroux Books for Young Readers
An imprint of Macmillan Publishing Group, LLC
120 Broadway, New York 10271 • fiercereads.com

Our books may be purchased in bulk for promotional, educational,
or business use. Please contact your local bookseller or Macmillan
Corporate and Premium Sales Department at (800) 221-7945 ext.
5442 or by email at MacmillanSpecialMarkets@macmillan.com.

Library of Congress Cataloging-in-Publication Data is available.

First edition, 2023
Designed by Trisha Previte
Printed in the United States of America

ISBN 978-0-374-39099-0

1   3   5   7   9   10   8   6   4   2

This book is dedicated to the more than four hundred Ukrainian children killed by Russian forces since February 2022—and to the thousands who have been orphaned, abducted, or otherwise separated from their families; may they all find their way home

I'll Tell You No Lies

ONE

MOM DIED ON MONDAY MORNING, June 6, 1955, about half an hour after she dropped me off at school in Kaiserslautern.

Everything after the crash—everything in the four weeks between Ramstein and New York City—was just a blur in my head, but I remembered that morning very clearly. It was raining; I remembered because I came downstairs in sandals and had to go back up for different shoes. It was the eleventh anniversary of D-Day, the day we stormed the beaches at Normandy—though of course Dad didn't storm any beaches; he was flying sorties with Bomber Command, smashing German coastal defenses from the air. I would have remembered about D-Day anyway because I was writing about Martha Gellhorn, the war correspondent and the only woman to go ashore with the invasion force, for my final paper in Mr. Spencer's English class.

But the thing that really mattered about that morning was that it was the last Monday of the school year, the last full day of classes before graduation, and Mom had offered to let me ditch and go shopping with her in Mannheim instead.

She was lonely at Ramstein. Most of the other senior officers' wives were rich or college-educated or both, especially the intelligence officers' wives, and Mom was a farm kid from central Ohio who had worked a factory job during the war. She didn't have very many friends at Ramstein—real friends, I mean, close friends—and in a few weeks she wouldn't have me. We had made plans for me to spend the summer with Uncle Fred and Aunt Jean in the States, "reacclimating," before the start of my fall term at college in Pennsylvania.

I turned her down. I had four years of perfect attendance records; I hadn't even taken a sick day. I had already been accepted to Bryn Mawr, contingent on my final report card; and my marks were good enough; and I was admittedly such a teacher's pet that cutting one day wasn't going to change a thing, but I was proud of those attendance records. I was the sort of person who was proud of attendance records. Mom was the sort of person who would phone the school office with some made-up story about a dead great-aunt and spring me from classes for the day. She always told people I was more grown-up than she was. She was just eighteen when she had me—she and Dad married young, as people did in rural Ohio in the Depression—and I think she tended to think of herself more as my fun older sister, or maybe as my bad-apple friend, than as my mother.

She crashed on Autobahn 6 on the way into Mannheim. She was dead before the ambulance got there.

I was still alive because I had turned her down.

I thought about that a lot. The base chaplain at Ramstein said that was called survivor's guilt, but I didn't really feel guilty. I was just angry at how stupid it was. You were supposed to believe everything happened for a reason, there was no such thing as random chance, but the only reason I could see was this was God's way of telling me I had done the right thing by not ditching class, and that was a stupid reason.

THREE WEEKS AFTER THE CRASH, Dad got our clearances for a Military Air Transport Service flight from West Germany to New York City and said we were moving back to the States.

He told me he had been ordered to report to a new station—Griffiss Air Force Base in Rome, New York. The clearances were for the following Monday, the Fourth of July; we had one week to pack. He didn't tell me until we had touched down at Idlewild early on Tuesday morning that they wanted him at Griffiss immediately. In fact, they were sending a special transport plane, a Convair Samaritan, to take us up directly. That was VIP treatment. Normally they would just have us take a train or bus.

He told me this as we stood there alone on the Idlewild apron in the predawn half-light, waiting for our three suitcases and the cardboard box with Mom's ashes, the city looming in the distance. The MATS flight had been empty except for the two of us and the five members of the flight crew, which in retrospect I should have noticed as unusual.

As if on cue, the promised Samaritan taxied up, propellers spiraling slowly out of sync.

I was stunned speechless, first. Up until that moment, I assumed we were taking Mom's ashes back to Ohio. I hadn't thought about it; I had just assumed. Both sets of grandparents were buried at Saint Joseph Cemetery in Columbus. I had just assumed we would be going to Columbus to put Mom's ashes in the family plot before we went on to the new station.

Then I was angry.

I could take the rest of it—a week to pack seven years of our lives into suitcases, twenty hours of traveling. I didn't care. But I thought they would give us time to bury her.

"I could go," I said to Dad. We were alone in the cabin; once again we were the only ones on the plane except for the flight crew. We had been sitting in silence since takeoff. The only sounds were the drone of the engines and the steady, oddly comforting thrum of the propellers. The Manhattan skyline sparkled in pink-and-gold morning sunlight below us.

Dad said, "What?" He was looking over some papers in a file folder spread open on his lap. He had been looking over those same papers since Frankfurt. He hadn't slept a wink. Every time I looked over, he had his reading lamp on and that folder open. He kept flipping slowly through the pages one by one, coming to the end of the stack, starting over again. It was some sort of personnel file; I could see a photograph clipped on the first page. I had no idea whether he was actually reading it or just looking at it to keep his mind off things.

"I could go to Columbus," I said. "I could stay with Uncle Fred and Aunt Jean. They were planning for me to come anyway."

"We'll both go," Dad said, thumbing a page over, not looking up, "or we'll find someplace up here."

"She would want to be in Columbus." As far as I knew, the only time Mom had ever been to New York was when we changed planes through Idlewild on the way to Germany seven years ago. She had never been upstate. Rome, New York, wouldn't mean anything to her. I hated the thought of leaving her ashes in a place that didn't mean anything.

"So we'll both go," Dad repeated, "as soon as I'm done with this."

"What does that mean, when you're done?"

"As soon as this assignment's done."

"When is the assignment going to be done?"

"Couple of days."

"Then I don't see why I couldn't just go ahead and—"

"No," he said, in a tone that said *And that's that*—and it struck me in that moment that he must have been the one who requested we go straight to Griffiss.

I should have put it together. I should have known from that empty MATS flight. They wouldn't have flown us out on the Fourth of July unless Dad had put in the request himself.

He had done the same thing seven years ago. He had packed us up and moved us to Germany less than a month after Grandma died. Everybody has their own way with grief, the base chaplain at Ramstein said, and this was Dad's—to throw himself into a new project, to lose himself absolutely in his work. I should have put it together.

He must have felt the anger in my silence. He looked up from his papers, his face softening just a little.

"It's just for a couple of days, Shel. They need me to deal with this. Just for a couple of days. Then we'll go. I'll take some leave days, and we'll go out to Columbus. Okay?"

"Okay," I whispered.

He hesitated. I thought for a moment he was going to say something else, but he didn't. He just reached across the seat arm and took my hand. He did it slowly, stiffly, a little self-consciously; it wasn't the sort of thing that came naturally to him. But he held on tight. His hands were strong and callused—working-class hands, unexpected for an intelligence officer, a guy with a desk job. He hadn't started in the ACTS, the officers' school. He had earned his commission during the war as an enlisted airman.

He held my hand for the rest of the hour-long flight. I fell asleep at some point and didn't wake up until I heard the bump and *whir* of the landing gear opening beneath us, and in the meantime he had gone back to looking at those papers on his lap. But he hadn't let go of my hand.

THEY HAD A RENTAL CAR waiting for us on the apron at Griffiss. Dad drove me out to the housing development, Birchwood Park, and let me off in the driveway with the house key, the suitcases, and the box with Mom's ashes. Then he went back up to base. He promised he would be back for dinner. We would dress up and go downtown and find something nice. My first real, grown-up American dinner. I had been eleven years old when we moved to Germany.

The house was brand-new—small and modest, two bedrooms and two baths all on a single floor in ranch style, but so new the paint still looked wet. I left the luggage on the front stoop and spent a little while walking through the empty rooms, switching on lights and looking in closets and pulling up the ugly preinstalled aluminum blinds so I could open the windows. The air was thick and heavy with the chemical smell of new carpet. This was a new development, Birchwood Park. We were one of the first families to move in; most of the other lots were empty. The unfinished cul-de-sac stopped dead in the tall yellow Indian grass just past our house. A long, snaking arm of woods lay beyond—somber, ancient pines and silvery gray birches—and then the river, the Mohawk, running southward to join the Erie Canal. The names—Mohawk River, Erie Canal—were all something out of history books or James Fenimore Cooper. This house felt wrong here—ugly and modern and out of place. *I* felt wrong here. I felt the odd need to walk on tiptoes in this house, as if I were an intruder.

The girl came walking up out of the woods while I was wrestling the last suitcase over the threshold. She walked out of the grass and paused on the sparkling asphalt pavement, brushing at her slacks and inspecting each ankle one after the other—being careful about ticks, I supposed. She was carrying one of those boxed watercolor sets in her hand and a light-weight traveling easel in a case on her shoulder.

"Hello!" she called to me, and then she came running over at a smooth, easy little jog, holding on to her impressively brimmed sun hat with her free hand. "Hello. How do you do?" she said again when she got closer, letting go of the hat to extend that slim, manicured hand to me. Sunlight flashed on the lenses of her Aviators. "I'm Jo. Jo Matheson."

For a moment, I just gaped at her. She looked as if she had stepped right out of the summer issue of *Vogue*, certainly not as if she had just stepped out of the woods behind my house. She wore a gauzy, sleeveless white blouse—tied up about the waist so you could see just a peek of tanned midriff—and trim tan slacks and Capezio flats. Her sleek, dark hair, framing her rather sharp elfin face beneath the hat, was fashionably short and tousled, like an Italian starlet's—the Gina Lollobrigida look, if Gina Lollobrigida were for some reason wandering around the woods of upstate New York.

"I saw your car," she explained. "I was down at the river."

I swept a useless hand over my rumpled skirt and an equally useless hand through my blond bob, plastered a smile on, and took her hand, feeling flushed and sticky and ungraceful.

"Shelby Blaine," I said.

"Shelby." The girl, Jo, gave me a quick, brilliant smile as she squeezed my fingers and dropped them. "That was your—"

"Dad—yes. Colonel Robert Blaine. He's with intelligence at the base. Or he will be. We just got here."

"He must be here because of that pilot," she said.

"The pilot?"

"The Russian."

She must have seen the sheer confusion on my face.

"That's all right," she said. "The only reason I know anything about it is because I'm supposed to throw a party for him."

"A party for a Russian pilot," I repeated stupidly.

"Oh—he's a defector. He's here for a debriefing or something. They're sending him up from Washington, and I'm supposed to give him a party. You know—show him how we do it in the free world. I'm chair of the base events committee."

I wouldn't in a million years have pegged her as "chair of the base events committee." I wasn't sure how old she was. She was one of those people who could believably be anywhere from eighteen to thirty. But "chair of the base events committee" brought up mental pictures of a stiff, grim, tight-mouthed older lady, a senior officer's wife, who wore boxy tweed suits and outdated netted hats with fake cherries and who looked as if she disapproved of the world in general and girls in midriff tops and slacks in particular.

"Dad didn't say anything about a Russian pilot," I said carefully, turning this over in my head. He hadn't told me anything at all about this assignment. It was important enough that Mom's funeral could wait while he dealt with it; that was all I knew.

"Well, that's probably why he's with intelligence and I'm chair of the events committee," Jo said. "He can keep his mouth shut." She eyed me and seemed to come to a belated realization. "You're here all by yourself?"

"It's me and Dad."

Her gaze traveled past me through the open doorway to linger on our three sad suitcases and the box with Mom's ashes. "Where have you come from?"

"West Germany. Ramstein. Dad just transferred."

"I'm sorry. I don't mean to grill you," she said. "I'm sure you want to nap or something."

"That would be nice," I agreed a little coolly.

"When do your things get here?"

"Things?"

"Your furniture and things." She was still looking pointedly at the suitcases.

I had no idea. I remembered Dad talking to somebody over the phone about furniture last week, but I had no idea what arrangements he had made, or with whom. He hadn't said a word about furniture when he let me off just now.

"I think they're supposed to be bringing the furniture today," I said.

Jo wasn't going to be put off so easily. "What are you going to eat?"

"Eat?"

"You haven't got a thing. What are you going to eat? Have you even got linens—towels—anything?" She tipped her sunglasses down to study me. "He just *left* you here?"

"We're eating dinner out."

"What a guy." She shoved the sunglasses back on. "Look, I'll tell you what. I'll run home and get the car—I'm just the next cul-de-sac over. We'll go downtown and get you some lunch and an ungodly amount of coffee, and then we'll stop by Tahan's and see about your furniture delivery. Can't believe he just dropped you on the curb and left you. Give me ten minutes."

I opened my mouth. She shot me a withering glare, eyebrows arching.

"Ten minutes," she repeated. "You're not allowed to say no."

TWO

TWELVE MINUTES LATER, WE WERE in Jo's cherry-red Bel Air convertible, speeding into downtown Rome.

Jo Matheson—Mrs. Lieutenant Colonel George Matheson—was twenty-four years old. Everybody always expected something scandalous, she said, but there wasn't anything scandalous. He was a thirty-five-year-old bachelor, she had been a graduate student at Rochester Institute of Technology, and they met last year at some officers' charity function or other. But she liked letting people think there was something scandalous. It gave them something to talk about, and God knew they needed that in Rome.

She was, I gathered, bored out of her mind.

She had a graduate degree in mechanical engineering. I wasn't exactly sure what that was, but it sounded impressive, and I told her so, being polite.

She snorted a little laugh.

"Can't do anything with it. Who's going to hire a woman engineer? Not the Air Force—not an officer's wife. I should have put the money toward Patricia Duncan's Finishing School. At least then I'd actually know how to play bridge." She swung the Bel Air neatly into a parking spot in front of a department store called Goldberg's. "The extent of my responsibilities," she said. "Friday afternoon bridge club and dinner parties."

The Russian's party was tomorrow night, seven o'clock, at the Officers' Club on base. It was mostly a publicity thing, she explained. All the top Griffiss brass would be there, and some State Department people up from Washington, and a press team hoping to get permission to write him up in a special report. But it could be a sort of welcome party for Dad and me too.

"So you'd better come," she said. "How old are you anyway?"

"Eighteen."

"Good. Old enough to drink in New York State," she said. "That's the only way to make it through these things."

She paid for my egg salad sandwich and iced coffee at the Goldberg's lunch counter. I didn't have any American money. I had been too flustered to remember to exchange my deutsche marks at the Finance Office at Ramstein before we left, and there hadn't been time this morning at Idlewild. I said I would pay her back. She gave me another of those withering glares.

"Please," she said.

We sat at the counter. She was tall enough, even in those flats, for her feet to reach the footrest on the bar. I wasn't. I sat with my saddle shoes dangling, like a gawky little kid. We would have made an interesting study in contrasts if there had been anybody to study us. We had the place to ourselves. It was about ten o'clock, not yet lunch hour. It was already oppressively hot. The sun was beating in through the big plate glass window at the storefront. Even with the box fan graciously turned our way by the server, I was sweating. Ninety-four degrees today, the radio in the rental car said, one of the hottest days on record—one degree short of the all-time high.

Ninety-four degrees Fahrenheit was thirty-four degrees Celsius. I had to make the conversion in my head—minus thirty-two, times five, divided by nine. I didn't think I would ever stop having to make the conversion. I thought in Celsius and the metric system. I kept saying *danke* to the porters on the apron at Idlewild.

Jo looked cool as a cucumber, sipping gracefully at her coffee while I tried not to scoff my sandwich whole. I hadn't eaten since dinner on the MATS flight.

"So," she said. "Eighteen. Rough time to change stations, isn't it? You've got a life by eighteen."

I swallowed a mouthful of egg salad. I knew she was just being polite, making conversation, the way I had made conversation about her engineering degree, so I couldn't really be honest. I couldn't tell her just how rough. *Yes—Mom died a month ago, and Dad and I haven't talked since then.* You couldn't say that kind of thing to somebody over an egg salad sandwich at a lunch counter, not somebody you had just met, even if she was the only person in this whole country you knew.

I supposed I should be thankful she hadn't asked about boys. That seemed to be the only way people knew how to make conversation with a girl once she started wearing a bra: "So, are you seeing anybody?" But I sort of wished she had. Talking about boys would be easier.

"It wasn't too bad," I said. "The school term was already over. And I was coming back here for college anyway—back to the States, I mean."

"Where?"

"Bryn Mawr."

"Just 'coming back here for college,' she says. Bryn Mawr! That isn't just *college*. What are you going to do?"

Not "What do you want to do?" but "What are you going to do?"—as if there were no question I could do it, whatever it was. It was an important and, I thought, rather wistful distinction coming from a girl with a degree in mechanical engineering who was stuck hosting bridge clubs and dinner parties.

I decided I liked Jo a lot, even if she was just being polite.

"Journalism," I said around another mouthful.

"Foreign correspondent for *Collier's*," she said, nodding. "I can see it."

I stared at her, the lump of egg salad caught in my throat, and she gave me an arch little grin. I had the sudden feeling that she could see all the way through me—right through all the polite and proper layers to the real girl, the real Shelby Blaine, who was sharp and bitter and angry and whose mother's ashes were currently in a box on the living room floor.

"Come on," she said. "You want to be Martha Gellhorn writing for *Collier's*. She was a Bryn Mawr alumna, wasn't she?"

"So was Emily Kimbrough. Maybe I want to be Emily Kimbrough."

Jo finished her drink, scooped up an ice cube with the sugar spoon, and chewed it contemplatively. "You don't want to be Emily Kimbrough."

"Why not?"

"One—because I can't see you doing nice little pieces on the spring collections from Paris for *Ladies' Home Journal*."

She pushed her glass across the counter. "And two—because nobody who wants to be Emily Kimbrough is still wearing saddle shoes and bobby socks in the year of our Lord 1955."

AT THE FURNITURE STORE, TAHAN'S, the clerk said they were just loading up the delivery truck now—"Blaine, right? 102 Parkside? Scheduled for eleven o'clock?"—so back we sped in the Bel Air so I could be there to let them in.

"What a guy, your dad!" Jo yelled over the wind. "He could have told you!"

I pretended not to hear. I opened my handbag on my lap and made a show of digging for the house key. She had the needle pushing sixty miles per hour. I wasn't exactly sure what the conversion rate was between miles and kilometers, but sixty felt very fast on this potholed two-lane road that ran east-west between downtown and the base. In my mind's eye, the car kept missing corners, careening off the road, smashing into trees or sides of buildings in a tangle of twisted metal and burnt rubber and our own bloody bodies.

It took me three tries to open the door when we got to the house; my hands were still shaking. I knew Jo must have noticed, but she just said easily, "Good for you—locking up. I should get in the habit. We were in base housing till last month, and I never locked up on base. I keep forgetting Birchwood isn't technically on base."

"We lock up on base too," I said. "Dad doesn't believe in leaving doors unlocked."

"Intelligence officers," Jo said knowingly. The Tahan's truck was pulling up to the curb. "Well, he doesn't have to worry.

This is Rome, New York. It's like living in Grover's Corners. Everybody knows everybody."

They brought in the furniture. Dad must have just told the store shopper to pick everything out for us. It was all the sort of ultramodern stuff that he hated and that Mom would dog-ear in catalogs for him as a joke: chairs and tables of bright cinnamon-colored pecan wood, spindly legs splayed at angles; cushions and pillows in garish green and yellow and turquoise. There were two bedroom sets—exactly identical, one full bed and one dresser apiece—and a dining set for the kitchen and three pieces for the living room: sofa, coffee table, armchair. There were two boxes of kitchenware and linens—the essentials only, pots, pans, two place settings with flatware, two sets of bath towels, two sets of sheets. Everything else I would need to get at the post exchange on base.

Jo took the new linens home to wash and dry on her line. We had a washer, part of the fitted kitchen, but no clothesline. Jo went outside and checked. I wouldn't have thought to.

There were so many things I hadn't thought about—dish towels, groceries, a telephone hookup. I had the feeling Dad hadn't thought about them either. At least somebody had gotten the memo to turn on our electricity and water.

Mom would have thought about things like this. Mom would *know* to think about things like this.

"I miss you so much," I said aloud into the silence, standing there alone in that strange new living room in that strange new house. There was an ache under my ribs; there was a knot in my throat.

Dad got back at about half past six. Jo had dropped off the towels and bedding, crisp and fresh from the line. I was in the armchair with *Homage to Catalonia*. Most of my books had gone in donations to the base library at Ramstein, but I kept the first-edition Orwell and the collected Agatha Christie I got at Hatchards bookshop when Mom and I went to London last year. I had put on my sensible old pencil dress, the navy one with the little bolero jacket, fairly dull but quality enough to serve as a dinner dress. I couldn't bring myself to touch the cocktail dress Mom had picked out for me for my birthday back in May—my first real, grown-up cocktail dress, sophisticated and dramatic in dark sea-green silk shantung. It was still in tissue paper in its box in my suitcase. I wasn't sure I could ever bring myself to touch it.

Dad came in the door and stopped short.

"You're already dressed," he said.

He had his briefcase in one hand and a brown paper bag and two Coca-Cola bottles in the other. He shut the door with a foot and gave me an apologetic half grimace, half grin.

"I was beat," he said. "I'm sorry. I just got us something from the commissary."

And it wasn't fair of me to be sore, I knew it wasn't fair of me to be sore—not about something as stupid as dinner, not when I knew he hadn't slept on the flights. But God knew it wasn't just about dinner. It was dinner and everything else. It was dinner and a month's worth of things he hadn't thought to tell me first. It was that furniture delivery; it was that special transport plane already waiting for us at Idlewild this morning. It was this assignment; it was this whole change of station.

This was his way with grief—I knew. I *knew*. But he hadn't once paused to consider whether it was mine.

"It's fine," I said.

"I'll make it up," he said. "Tomorrow night?"

"There's something on base tomorrow night," I said cuttingly.

"We don't have to go to that." He put the bag and bottles on the coffee table.

"I do. I met Mrs. Matheson today—the events committee lady." I dug into the bag to investigate. There were two cold sandwiches in deli paper. "She washed our sheets. I owe her."

He took off his uniform cap and dropped onto the sofa. "That was nice of her," he said. "It looks good—everything. Looks really good." He waved the cap vaguely around the room, making a broad sweep with his arm. "We need some pictures or something."

"Well, she wants me to come to her party." I concentrated on unwrapping the deli paper. "She said there's some Russian being sent up here from Washington."

He was loosening his necktie, his cap on his knee. His hands went still. I could feel him stiffen.

Slowly, he pulled off the tie and draped it on the table.

"They wanted me to do the debriefing," he admitted.

"It couldn't be anybody else? It had to be you?"

"I was working on a new MiG at Ramstein—pulling together intelligence on a new MiG design." He leaned his elbows on his knees, resting his face in his hands. "We weren't sure it was anything beyond some schematics. Well, this guy was flying one. It got blown to hell when he was shot down, but he was flying one. They figure I know the questions to ask."

"And you couldn't question him at Ramstein? They had to send him to Rome, New York?"

"Griffiss's base mission is research and development. Command wanted Griffiss's R and D people in on the debriefing." Dad scrubbed his hands over his face and looked up. "Okay—so, Thursday night," he said. "We'll do dinner Thursday night, okay?"

I didn't care about dinner, and I didn't care about Jo Matheson's party, and it hurt that he thought I did—of all the things I could care about. But I had won my stupid little victory.

"Okay," I said.

"I'm sorry, Shel," he said.

I finished unwrapping the deli paper. They were egg salad sandwiches.

"It's fine," I said.

THREE

I SPENT MOST OF THE next day, Wednesday, on the bus, making trips back and forth from Birchwood to base—to the Identification Office to get photographed and fingerprinted for my base pass; to the commissary for groceries and cleaning supplies; to the post exchange for things like kitchen towels and place mats and drinking glasses. The clerk at the exchange register smiled at me as she wrapped up the glasses in paper.

"For your trousseau?" she asked.

I stared at her for a moment before it occurred to me that everything I had put on the counter was, of course, the sort of staple household stuff you would put in a hope chest—the sort of stuff you would be buying when you started out in your first house in your first station and would typically have no need to buy again while you were doing your ten years or so of Air Force service. Most people weren't trying to make a complete fresh start when they changed stations. Most people traveled with more than three suitcases.

I returned her smile as cordially as I could. My stomach was tight. I didn't want to have to explain.

"No, we just transferred from overseas. We were trying to travel light."

"The baggage allowances aren't nearly enough." She nodded in commiseration. "Where overseas?"

"We were at Ramstein. West Germany."

"I keep hoping for a Europe posting," she said a little wistfully. "But you'll like Griffiss. We've got a lot here—for being in the middle of nowhere, New York." She laughed. "Which flight is your husband's? Have you registered with the Wives' Club yet?"

"It's my dad," I said lightly. "I'm Shelby—Colonel Blaine's daughter. He's with intelligence."

"Oh," she said, "oh—I see! Well, tell your mother it's Building 406—the Officers' Wives' Club."

"I'll tell her," I said, smiling.

"Building 406—right up Hill Road."

"I'll tell her."

It was past six by the time I got back to the house. Dad was there. He was in the living room in his formal evening dress uniform, the summer-tan one with all his ribbons across the chest. I came up short in the doorway, and he gave me a quick grin. He was tying his bow tie, his cap under his arm.

"Shoe's on the other foot," he said. "Look who isn't dressed yet."

Somehow, I managed to shut the door. I put my shopping bags on the kitchen counter. The only time I ever saw him wear that uniform was for the Air Force Ball each September. Most of the other summer socials didn't require the full-dress uniform—and Dad avoided the socials anyway unless it was his squadron's turn to host, and even then Mom practically had to drag him. She had loved parties and dinner dances. She had lived for the Ball each year.

I didn't know how to do it. I didn't know how to stand it. Everywhere I turned, I came face-to-face with another reminder that she was gone.

"We don't have to go," I said.

His hands paused. "I thought you wanted to go."

"We don't have to."

He was silent for a moment, studying me. "Probably good to put in an appearance," he said. "Meet some people." He resumed tying his tie. "Don't want to get on Mrs. Matheson's bad side."

I didn't say anything. I didn't honestly think Jo Matheson cared one way or another whether we showed up to her party. She didn't strike me as the type to care about things like etiquette or social obligations. After all, she had put her money toward an engineering degree, not Patricia Duncan's Finishing School. But I had dug myself into a hole, and I was too proud to admit it.

"You want to leave after dinner, we'll leave," Dad said. He was silent, finishing with his tie, then he said quietly, "You should wear the green dress."

The green dress—the new dress, my birthday present. I shouldn't have been surprised he remembered. He had seen it once, the day we bought it, and hadn't said anything more than "Looks good" in that offhand, distracted way, but I knew better than to assume he hadn't been paying attention. He always paid attention, even when you could swear he was a million miles away. He caught everything.

"I need to get it fitted," I said.

"Oh," he said. "We'll have to find someplace in town."

"Yes."

He didn't say another word about the dress. He seemed a

little embarrassed to have brought it up in the first place. But I knew he could tell I was lying. He caught everything, and he was very good at parsing lies. I supposed that was why he was with intelligence.

I WAS RIGHT ABOUT JO Matheson.

They called her name from the bandstand after dinner. They were thanking the Twenty-Seventh Fighter-Interceptor Squadron Wives' Club and the events committee for hosting tonight, and they had floral arrangements for all the club and committee ladies by way of appreciation. A lean, sandy-haired man with oak leaf insignia on his collar—Colonel Matheson himself, I presumed—stood up quickly to take Jo's flowers for her, smiling in embarrassment and murmuring something inaudible to the emcee.

She hadn't even come. It would have stung more if I had cared at all about being there.

I was alone at our empty table. Dad had gone over to the bar to get us champagne. Dinner had been suffocating. Our table companions were a blithely oblivious elderly couple—he a thirty-year veteran who kept trying to get Dad to talk about the war, she a smiling saint with a halo of bluish white hair who asked me if there was a young gentleman. I told her there wasn't a young gentleman. She wished their grandson Eddie the Third could be here to meet me. They were a three-generation Air Force family—not many people could say that, could they? Eddie Junior was at Dobbins in Georgia, and Eddie the Third was with a fighter wing in Japan. She could never remember the name of the place he was at—something *sawa* or *zawa.* Anyway, I would like him, Eddie the Third. It really was a pity he couldn't be here. She could give me his APO number if I would like; he always appreciated getting mail from the States.

Dad came to my rescue by mentioning some people he knew at Dobbins.

They left when the band started up the dance numbers. Dad stood up politely to say good night, holding Mrs. Eddie the First's chair. He gave me a look when they were gone.

"Champagne?"

"Please," I said a little too vigorously.

He nodded. "Then we'll go."

He was still at the bar twenty minutes later, cornered by a couple of other officers, and from the looks of it, he was going to be there for a while. They had already been through a beer apiece and were starting on a second round.

I went and got my own champagne. It was good to see him talking and laughing. It was the first time in a month I had seen him anything close to relaxed. And honestly—with the champagne and a chance to breathe—I didn't mind just sitting here at the table, listening and watching, not having to talk to anybody or put on a stupid smiling face.

From where I sat—far corner of the room, my back to the wall—I could catch a glimpse of the Russian every now and then. He was a few tables in toward the dance floor, flocked by press people with flashing cameras and Air Force people and anonymous but important-looking men in suits who I assumed had something to do with the State Department. I was curious to see him despite myself. My concept of Russians was a conflicting jumble cobbled together from *Anna Karenina*, *For Whom the Bell Tolls*, *Animal Farm*, wartime newsreels about Lend-Lease shipments, and of course the rather bombastic propaganda campaigns proclaiming the dangers of the Red Menace: THE AVERAGE AMERICAN IS PRONE TO SAY, "IT CAN'T HAPPEN HERE." MILLIONS OF PEOPLE IN OTHER COUNTRIES USED TO SAY THE SAME THING. TODAY, THEY ARE DEAD—OR LIVING IN COMMUNIST SLAVERY. "Russians," to my mind, were both tragically noble and terrifyingly fanatical. This guy didn't look much of either. He was a bit younger than Dad—early thirties, I guessed. He was wearing civilian clothes, though his dark blond hair was in a military-style crew cut. He mostly looked annoyed. His jacket and tie were off, his sleeves rolled up, in open defiance of the dress code. His stony face was fixed in a scowl. He had been sitting there answering questions from that press team all night. He was probably having to do it all from a script too. I couldn't imagine those anxiously hovering State Department guys would risk letting him say just anything he wanted.

There was a part of me that couldn't help wondering whether he ever regretted defecting. What a nightmare life—to be trotted out like some kind of circus attraction. What a nightmare if this life truly was better than whatever he had left behind.

Better if he had just stayed in Russia. Better for all of us.

I drained my glass and set it down.

The only other person not involved with the Russian, the bar, or the dance floor was the boy a couple of tables over. He wasn't facing me; he was sort of in profile, watching the dancing with rapt attention. But he was directly between me and the Russian, and every time I looked over, the boy must have felt it peripherally and thought I was looking at him. It happened every single time. I would look over, and he would tilt his head slightly toward me, and then he would look quickly away again as if realizing his mistake.

Finally—sick of it, I supposed—he scraped his chair back and went over to the bar.

I nearly jumped when he reappeared suddenly at my elbow, holding another champagne coupe very carefully by the stem.

"Here—for you," he said politely, and proceeded to slosh every last drop of champagne out onto the tabletop as he set the coupe down.

It happened so quickly and unexpectedly that for a moment I couldn't react—just sat there mesmerized, watching the spilled champagne run to the edges of the table and down the sides of the long white tablecloth to puddle on the floor. Then I looked at him. His face was the picture of abject mortification: eyes wide, mouth open. His gaze met mine, horror-struck.

He snapped his mouth shut, swallowed, and squared his shoulders with the grim resolution of a martyr.

"I'll get another one," he said.

"Wait." A belated flash of understanding—he thought I was making eyes at him, asking him to refill my drink. "It's fine. Really, it's fine. I wasn't asking you—I wasn't trying to ask for another drink. I'm just waiting for my dad."

I regretted that the instant it was out of my mouth—"I'm waiting for my dad," as if I were eight years old—but he didn't really seem to hear anyway. He wasn't looking at me. He was looking at the bar with interest.

"Your dad," he repeated, as if he had just figured out how to fit this piece into the puzzle. "Colonel Blaine is your dad."

That caught me off guard. "How did you know that?"

"You came in together. You. Colonel Blaine." He spoke slowly, carefully, with a hint of an accent I couldn't place.

"No—I mean, how did you know he was Colonel Blaine?"

"Oh." He seemed to consider for a moment. "He asked the questions. At the debriefing today, he asked the questions."

Another belated flash of understanding. That accent. Debriefing.

I stared at him.

He darted a sidelong glance at me. His mouth pursed a little. "The . . . interrogation?" he offered hesitantly. "They call it 'debriefing.'"

"You're the Russian," I said, and he gave me a swift grin—an absolute gift of a grin, broad and dimpled and lovely. His eyes were warm, golden brown, the color of honey. His dark hair was cut rather aggressively short, shaved nearly to the scalp on the sides and only a bit longer on top, like a Boy Scout's rather imperfect summer-camp attempt at a Mohawk. It made him look very young for a pilot.

"The Ukrainian," he said. "Not the Russian. We are not the same. Is it okay?"

He had a hand on the back of Mrs. Eddie the First's empty chair.

The little edge of resentment inside me, blunted against his sheer unexpectedness, went cold and sharp again.

"Do girls usually fall for it?"

His brow creased. "Fall for it?"

"You know—the act. Spilling the drink as a conversation starter."

He was silent, holding a hand on the chair, looking at me with that puzzled crease in his brow, and it wasn't his fault. It wasn't his fault Dad had to do his debriefing, and it wasn't his fault Mom was dead.

"Forget it. Sit down if you want to sit down. I don't care."

He took the seat a little uncertainly. "I will get you another drink," he offered.

"I don't want another drink. I was making a joke."

"Oh," he said, and gave me another brilliant grin. I could tell he was still trying to work it out in his head.

"So who is that?" I asked him. "I thought he was you."

He followed my look over to the other table.

"No, he's Jones. CIA. My, um . . . my handler? They call him my handler. Like luggage. I have handlers so I don't get lost." Another grin. "He answers the questions for me—the newspaper questions. My English isn't very good yet."

"It seems pretty good to me." It was, in fact, incredibly good. I wondered how he had managed to learn. I doubted he got it in school. Maybe pilots were allowed to take English courses? From what I heard, the Reds treated their MiG pilots the way we treated movie stars.

It would explain things. It would explain his expectant hand on that chair. He was probably used to flashing that dimpled grin and getting whatever he wanted from girls.

"Jones tells the reporters my English isn't very good yet," he clarified. "He doesn't like me to talk to reporters. For security. Always security."

"Are you supposed to be talking to me?"

"Are you a reporter?"

"Not yet."

His brow dipped into that puzzled crease again.

"I'll be majoring in journalism," I told him.

"In the university," he said.

"Yes—in September."

"Then it's okay," he said. "I can talk to you until September. What's your name?"

"Shelby."

"Shelby," he repeated, as though testing the sound of it. "My name is Maksym Ivanovych." He smiled. "My American name."

"American name?"

"They made a mistake," he said. "On my American citizenship papers, they said Maksym Ivanovych. They made a mistake. They thought Ivanovych was the, um . . . the surname? The family name. Like you are Blaine. But it isn't my family name. It's my father's name—Ivan. That's how Ukrainian names are. You have your name, and your father's name, and your family name. Three names."

I wasn't sure I followed. "So what's your family name?"

"Kostyshyn," he said. "Maksym Ivanovych Kostyshyn. It means 'Ivan's son'—Ivanovych. There are lots of Ivanovyches because there are lots of Ivans. Lots of Maksym Ivanovyches in Ukraine." He shrugged. "In America, it's okay if I'm Maksym Ivanovych. There aren't so many. And Jones says maybe it's good the family name isn't on my papers."

"For security."

"For security," he echoed. "So. It's okay." He was watching the dance floor. It was a softer, more bittersweet number now:

Ask me no questions,
and I'll tell you no lies;
ask me no questions,
and there'll be no goodbyes.

"Do you dance like this?" he asked.

"What?"

"Like this." He swept a hand toward the floor.

"You mean swing?"

"Swing, yes. Do you swing?"

One last belated realization: He wanted to dance with me. He had come over with that drink because he was angling for a dance.

I couldn't answer, tongue-tied with sudden panic, and he rubbed one palm uncertainly with a thumb. "I thought maybe if you would like—"

"I can't."

It came out more sharply than I meant, and he drew back just a little. My face went hot. "I can't. This dress . . ." I was wearing my navy pencil again. I shifted my legs to the side so he could see the close, tapered fit of the skirt. My tongue still wouldn't cooperate. "Not really a good dancing dress."

He looked at my legs for half a heartbeat. He looked so very lost that I couldn't help but wonder whether this was the first time he had ever been rejected. But he nodded once, slowly and gravely.

"Okay," he said.

The CIA man, Jones, loomed suddenly over the table, and Maksym jumped up as if he had been kicked. "Hello, Mr. Jones."

Jones's tanned, stony face was still set in a scowl, but he gave me a courteous little nod. He was worrying a toothpick absently between his teeth. I could see him assessing the whole scene piece by piece—the empty glasses, the spilled champagne, the flush in my face, the way Maksym shot out of that chair—and arriving at exactly the wrong conclusion.

"Is he bothering you?"

He had to ask; I knew he had to ask. He couldn't afford his tame Russian misbehaving at a publicity event. But it still rubbed me the wrong way. It seemed pettily hurtful to ask the question when Maksym was standing right there and could understand English perfectly well. If Maksym *had* been bothering me, I could have told him off myself. I didn't need the CIA to dump a boy for me.

I slid my legs back under the table.

"We were just talking," I said.

"She isn't a reporter," Maksym said. "She's Miss Blaine. It's okay."

Jones picked up Maksym's empty champagne coupe and studied it thoughtfully, as though he were collecting evidence from a murder scene. "Did you drink any of it?" he asked Maksym.

"No." Maksym made an expressive sweep with his hand. "On the floor—all of it."

"It was an accident," I said.

"Yes, an accident," Maksym agreed.

Jones set the coupe back down on the table. He ran another glance over me.

"Blaine," he said, chewing on his toothpick, "Blaine. You wouldn't happen to be—"

"My daughter," Dad said.

He had ventured over from the bar at some point. I hadn't even noticed. He rested his hands lightly but territorially on the back of my chair. "Is there a problem, Jones?"

I spent a split second wondering how they knew each other already—and evidently well enough to dislike each other—before it occurred to me that of course Jones, the handler, would be at the debriefing sessions too.

"Not yet," Jones said coolly. He gave me another little nod as he moved away, still playing with that toothpick. "Good night then, Miss Blaine." And to Maksym, jerking a thumb— "All right, let's go. We're done here."

"Good night, Shelby," Maksym said, smiling at me.

I SLIPPED OFF MY PUMPS in the darkness of the car, wincing. I hadn't worn heels in a long time. My feet and calves were aching, and identical blisters had sprung up on the outsides of my small toes. "What was all that about?" I asked Dad.

I thought he wasn't going to answer. He crooked an arm over the shoulder of his seat as he backed the car out of the parking space. We drove slowly and in silence from the Officers' Club to the west gate, and he lifted a hand to return the salutes from the gate sentries. Once on the road, it was about three minutes' driving time from the gate to the house in Birchwood.

He said finally, just before we turned onto the cul-de-sac, "Stay away from him."

"From—"

"From Jones."

His voice was cold and hard. I wasn't used to it from him. Dad was nothing if not unflappable. He nosed the car into the driveway and up under the carport. He cut the engine and sat for a moment, leaning his head back against the seat.

"He's a field agent," he said. "I called a contact down at the agency. He's not a handler—not trained as a handler. He was a field agent until three weeks ago, when he took this case. He doesn't have the qualifications to be handling a defector. He's on this case because he pulled strings to be on this case." He hesitated. "Or because somebody pulled strings for him to be on this case."

I absorbed this uneasily. There was a fist clenched in the pit of my stomach. "What does that mean? You think he's working for the Reds?"

Dad let out a breath. "He shouldn't be here; that's what I know. I want you to stay away from him."

He must have been spooked. I couldn't remember his ever speaking so much or so plainly about anything to do with his work—not to me. But I couldn't see that it mattered all that much—that is, to me personally. Obviously it mattered whether Agent Jones was secretly a Red. But I couldn't imagine I would be crossing paths with him again after tonight.

I felt around for my shoes in the dark. I wouldn't be crossing paths with Maksym Ivanovych Kostyshyn either, and there was a treacherous little part of me wishing I had given him that dance.

FOUR

JO SHOWED UP UNANNOUNCED IN the Bel Air a little after noon the next day and honked the horn from the curb.

"Get in," she called. "We're going to the lake."

She sat there with the engine idling, one arm slung over the driver's door and her manicured fingers tapping impatiently on the doorframe—as if I were being the difficult one—while I ran around the house gathering shoes and hat and handbag and suntan oil.

"I need an early-warning system," I said to her as I slid gingerly onto the hot buttercream leather of the passenger seat. It came out a little sharply; I couldn't help it. I hadn't really been cross at her last night, but I was cross that she could show up now acting as if last night hadn't happened.

She didn't seem to notice. "What you're talking about is called a telephone. You do need one. And this is Rome, New York. If you don't do something spontaneously, you're never going to do anything."

That was how we ended up at Delta Lake, which was—Jo said—technically a reservoir, not a lake, but everybody called it Delta Lake. It was about a ten-minute drive north of town, going by the state route, Highway 46. She had brought her watercolors. She came up here a lot to paint, she said, because on weekdays you pretty much had the place to yourself, even in the summer; everybody else went up to Lake Ontario or over to the Finger Lakes instead. She set herself up at the edge of the pinewood just above the water. There was a blue heron wading in the pebbly shallows below us.

"That's another thing," she said. "Find yourself a hobby if you want to stay sane."

I had shoved *Homage to Catalonia* into my handbag at the house, unthinking. I hadn't pulled it out yet. George Orwell had fought in a socialist militia in Spain. I didn't really think Jo would care. Dad didn't care. But I wasn't sure how well it reflected on him, my reading socialists, even if George Orwell had written polemics against the Reds and we all had to read *Animal Farm* for school. Everybody was treading carefully, afraid of being labeled a pinko, a commie sympathizer—especially in Air Force circles. Two years ago, an Air Force lieutenant lost his commission over his family's suspected communist sympathies. He had been reinstated only after Ed Murrow from CBS ran a special program on his case and brought it to worldwide attention. Not everybody was lucky enough to get an Ed Murrow special.

So I was just sitting there on a blanket in a leaf-mottled patch of sunlight, rubbing Coppertone on my legs and slapping at mosquitoes, trying not to scare away that heron.

"So you met him," Jo said. "The Russian."

I said, "How do *you* know?"

This time, she must have caught the edge in my voice. She gave me a quick, incisive look. "Before you get all hot and bothered, want to know how I spent my night? I was driving around buying up every bag of ice I could find between here and Boonville. Somebody tripped the breakers in the Club kitchen. The freezers had been off all day. *You* try putting on a dinner dance with a full bar and no ice. I don't want to hear it." She jabbed her brush at her paper with a vengeance. "But I do want to hear about the Russian, because *I* didn't get to meet him."

"All right," I said, "all right. I'm sorry."

"Anyway, I saw photos—that's how," she said. "One of my committee girls has a Polaroid. She snapped you. Don't tell anybody; I've got the feeling we weren't supposed to—snap him, I mean. But we needed shots for the committee newsletter, and I need proof for posterity that I threw a party for a Russian defector." She swiped another brushstroke. "So what happened?"

"We talked a little," I said guardedly. I didn't want to explain the whole thing—the mistaken looks, the spilled champagne. I didn't want her latching on to the fact that I had met Maksym only because he thought I was making eyes at him. I didn't trust her to believe I wasn't. Why else would he have come over to my table, after all?

"He spoke English? Or you mean through a translator?"

"No, he spoke English. Really well, actually. I mean—he had an accent, but he spoke it really well."

"I didn't think they learned English," Jo said. "Why would they need to? They're not allowed to leave Russia. Except for spies."

"I thought maybe the pilots learned it," I said. "In case—I don't know. In case they run across some of our planes in the air and have to speak over the radio. I imagine they've got to know some English."

"Well, George doesn't know Russian. Not that I know of," Jo said. "If we don't make our guys learn Russian, I doubt the Reds are making their guys learn English." She dabbed at her paper with the tip of her brush. "How was he?"

"He was nice."

Another look. "Is that the kind of reporting that gets you the Pulitzer? 'He was nice'? I need more than that."

"Nice, polite. I don't know."

"Well, let's start simple. Old? Young? You can't really tell from the photo. You can't really see his face."

"Pretty young, I think."

"Good-looking?"

I was glad for the heat and sunlight just then—glad that my cheeks were already flushed. I remembered that dimple in his grin very distinctly; I remembered the way he had carefully tested my name on his tongue. "Nice face but not very tall," I said, which was true. He had come barely to Agent Jones's chin when he stood up from the table last night.

"We can work with that," Jo said. "What's his name?"

"Maksym."

"Very Russian."

"He's Ukrainian. He did say that. Ukrainian, not Russian."

"I bet it's not his real name," Jo said. "I bet they just made it up for him—the CIA. Code name Maksym." She squinted at her paper critically and dabbed one more dot of paint. "All right—go on. What else did he say?"

I swatted a mosquito. "That was it. His handler came and got him—the CIA guy who looks after him. I don't think he was supposed to be talking to me."

"They don't trust him," Jo observed.

"Or they don't trust me."

"Think about it. They're never going to trust him. He switched sides. How do you trust the guy who switches sides?"

"He switched to *our* side," I said.

"That still makes him a traitor," Jo said. "Nobody trusts a traitor. If he switched sides once, he can do it again." She rinsed her brush. "Poor guy, whatever his name is. Probably just wanted a normal conversation for a change."

THE FIRST POLICE CAR CAME up behind us, siren blaring, just after we had turned off the highway. Jo was speeding again.

"Oh, come on—really?" she said, hastily downshifting and nosing the Bel Air onto the shoulder. "As if he doesn't have anything better to do with his time—and stop looking so self-righteous, Blaine. I wasn't even doing fifty. Give me that lipstick in my handbag."

The speed limit on this road, Floyd Avenue, the east-west road running from downtown Rome to Birchwood and then to base, was twenty-five miles per hour. I had made a point to look for it after she had done sixty the other day. But I didn't say anything. I gave her the lipstick. The police car dipped into the other lane and went right on past us without slowing.

"Well," Jo said, tube poised at her lips.

Two more police cars flew past, hurtling at full speed toward the base—and then a fourth, rounding the turn onto Floyd so sharply that the tires shrieked.

"Those are state troopers," Jo said. "Something's up."

She capped the lipstick, gave it back to me, checked over

her shoulder, and eased the Bel Air back onto the pavement. "I wonder if there's been an accident," she said in an uncharacteristically subdued kind of voice. She was gripping the wheel with both hands.

"There isn't any smoke," I said, leaning forward to look at the sky over the base. "If a plane had come down . . ."

"Right," she said shortly.

Then she said, "I hate it sometimes, you know? Being the Air Force wife. And it's almost worse having that stupid degree. It's worse *knowing*. I can tell you every single thing that could possibly go wrong with an R-3350 engine, and there's absolutely nothing I can do about it."

And I almost said something stupid.

I almost asked her whether Colonel Matheson took planes up very often. I couldn't imagine he did, being a senior officer. Dad certainly didn't. He had to log a certain number of hours per year to keep his certification current; that was it. Even if there had been a crash, it seemed highly unlikely that Colonel Matheson would have been involved, just by virtue of those oak leaves on his collar.

But of course that wasn't the point. Jo probably knew most of the pilots. She played bridge with their wives every Friday afternoon; she hostessed their dinner parties. It didn't matter whose plane came down. It was awful in any case.

It scared me a little—that my first reaction should be to wonder why she cared so much. What sort of cold, unfeeling person would wonder why she cared? When had I become that person?

We drove the rest of the way to Birchwood slowly and in silence.

There was an unfamiliar car sitting in our driveway—a sleek black sedan, ominous-looking somehow. Unease twisted in the pit of my stomach. It was wrong, all of it—that sedan, all those state troopers. "Do you know whose car that is?" I asked Jo.

"Looks like the G-men, doesn't it? Come to bust up that moonshine still you've got in your backyard. I told you to shut that operation down." She squinted through her Ray-Bans at the license plate, then put on the parking brake and killed the engine. "Here, I'll come with you."

Dad shoved open the screen door and came out onto the stoop while we were still making our way up from the street. Another man was with him. Just for a second, I thought he was the CIA man, Jones. He was dressed like Jones: black suit pants but no jacket, loosely knotted tie, crumpled white shirt, sleeves rolled up to the elbow in a losing battle against the heat. Same blunt scowl, though his hair was in a bristly flattop, not that government-issue crew cut. A fedora dangled from his finger-tips; a pair of browline glasses was slipping down his sweat-sheened nose. The gold badge clipped on his belt said FBI.

Stupidly, I thought of George Orwell in my handbag.

"This her?" the FBI man asked Dad.

"Yes," Dad said.

His face was blank—not just taut or drained, the way it always looked now, but dead blank. It knocked the breath out of me. I remembered that look.

One of the other officers' wives had to come get me at school in Kaiserslautern after the crash. She wouldn't tell me what was wrong—maybe she wasn't allowed to tell me, or maybe she just didn't want to be the one to tell me—and my first, panicked assumption was that something had happened to Dad. Something had happened at the base. Wild possibilities: A plane had come down and crashed right into his office block; a Red saboteur had planted a bomb. But of course I wouldn't have been the only one getting called home in that case. Rhine High was a Department of Defense school; 90 percent of the kids there were Air Force brats. An accident on base would affect all of us. So then my second assumption was that this was Mom playing an elaborate prank, determined to get me out of class. It never even occurred to me that something might have happened to her. All those wild possibilities—it never occurred to me to think about the mundane ones. But Dad was waiting at the house when I got there, and Mom was dead. It had been raining that morning; the roads were slick; the car had hydroplaned. She had lost control and slammed into one of those big concrete pylons beneath an overpass. It could have happened to anybody, and it happened to my mother.

He'd had this look on his face when he told me, this exact same look—as if a switch had been shut off somewhere inside him.

Jo had to ask. I couldn't.

"Is something wrong? We've been up at the lake." She marched past me and stuck out her hand briskly. "I'm Jo Matheson," she announced. "We haven't met."

She was talking to Dad, but the FBI man was the one who reached for her hand.

"Kimball, ma'am," he said, "Agent Kimball, Federal Bureau of Investigation." With effort, he rearranged his blocky face into what I imagined was supposed to be a smile. "Colonel

Blaine was expecting, uh, Shelby"—he flicked a glance in my direction—"at home. Got a little concerned about the empty house, that's all. Just being thorough."

I found my voice finally.

"You called the FBI?" I asked Dad.

"Oh—not on you, ma'am," Agent Kimball said. "We're looking for that Russian."

FIVE

THEY HAD BEEN LOOKING FOR him for six hours.

We got the story in bits and pieces from Agent Kimball, who had come up with an FBI team from the field office in Utica. Dad wouldn't say a word. There had been some question, it seemed, about Maksym's testimony—some part of his testimony that hadn't held up at the latest debriefing session this morning, evidently glaring enough to raise suspicions about whether any part of his story was actually true.

They had given him the chance to explain himself. He couldn't explain himself. They told him he would have twenty-four hours to reconsider his answers before they sent him back to Washington for another round of CIA interrogations, after which—if the CIA wasn't satisfied—they would be packing him off to Moscow in a prisoner exchange.

He had panicked.

He tried to fight, which went about as well as you could imagine, given that he was unarmed and Agent Jones had hand-to-hand combat experience from his time with special forces during the war. He ended up handcuffed to the bed in his dorm room on suicide watch. He had as good as confessed he was a Red agent by fighting instead of cooperating, Agent Kimball explained, and they were afraid he would try to silence himself before they could get any usable intelligence out of him. Agent Jones—Agent Kimball was rather contemptuous about this part—left him with an MP while he stepped out of the room to telephone the agency for further orders.

When he came back twenty minutes later, the bed was empty, the MP was unconscious and disarmed, the window was open, and Maksym was gone.

His room had been on the second floor of the dorm; the drop was straight down onto asphalt. Most people couldn't have jumped from that window and walked away—but of course Maksym, as a pilot, would be trained to make parachute jumps. Dad had made parachute jumps as part of his flight training during the war. Before you jumped from planes, you were jumping from towers and sliding down to the ground on cables, learning how to roll into your landing. If Maksym had handed himself down from the window ledge first, shortening the distance to the ground by a third, and if he had landed his fall just right—it was conceivable he could have walked away.

That had been about eleven o'clock, nearly an hour before Jo and I left for the lake. It was ten till five now.

There wasn't any reason for us to worry, Agent Kimball said; the fugitive had most likely left the immediate area. In any case, he would be avoiding places like Birchwood—residential areas, population centers. They were combing the woods, the roads, the river, the canal. They were watching all the bus and train stations. They had notified the Canadian border patrol at the Thousand Islands crossing, eighty miles north of here— just a precautionary measure. The fugitive wasn't going to make it to the border. He didn't know the lay of the land; he spoke with a distinctive accent; he had been injured when he attempted to fight. He would, by now, be getting increasingly desperate. He would start making mistakes.

They would find him. One way or another, they would deal with that Russian by nightfall.

DAD AND AGENT KIMBALL LEFT in Agent Kimball's car to go back up to base. Dad said the telephone company was supposed to be out within the hour to install our hookup. He wrote his office number on a scrap of paper and told me to call him when the phone was up. He would try to swing back by for dinner around six thirty, maybe seven.

His voice, as he said all of this, was perfectly neutral. He wasn't going to let anything slip in front of Agent Kimball, and of course he didn't have any choice but to go back up to base until he was given leave to do otherwise. But I could tell from his face how on edge he was. The empty house had shaken him badly.

I took his office number; I said I would call him. There didn't seem to be any point reminding him he had promised me dinner out tonight.

Jo walked over to the filling station on Floyd Avenue and came back with the evening paper. She laid it out on the coffee table so we could both look at it, and we sat there reading it silently between us while the technicians from the telephone company installed the handset in the kitchen.

MASSIVE MANHUNT UNDERWAY FOR RED AGENT, the headline shouted—and then underneath, still all in blaring capitals: AIR FORCE INTELLIGENCE REVEALS DEFECTOR AS SOVIET OPERATIVE.

That press team had gotten to write their special report after all.

There wasn't actually much about him—nothing at all of his home or his family or anything of a personal nature, and very little of his life before June 4 of this year, the date of his defection. He was a senior lieutenant in the Soviet Air Forces, and he had been a test pilot at the base in Kaliningrad, on the Baltic Sea—the part of Russia that belonged to Germany before the war. He had flown out of Kaliningrad that morning, June 4, and ejected from his badly damaged MiG jet over the Danish island of Bornholm. He had requested and been granted asylum in the United States, and he had been sent up here to Griffiss for debriefing with Air Force intelligence. There wasn't anything about how he had been caught out. Most of the article was taken up with reassurances to the public about the measures in place for capturing him—all probably just for show; they wouldn't broadcast the measures they were actually relying on—and instructions for contacting the FBI with any tips or leads.

There was a photograph though, dated June 24. He was grinning that dimpled grin and shaking hands with President Eisenhower. His naturalization papers, just signed, were laid out on the president's desk in the foreground. The caption said *Lieutenant Maksym Ivanovych was granted US citizenship in June by a special act of Congress.*

"They got his name wrong," I said.

"Hmm?"

"They got his name wrong."

"Didn't you say he was Maksym?"

"His last name. It isn't Ivanovych. He told me."

"Like I said—it's all just aliases," Jo said knowingly. "A spy isn't going to tell you his real name." She was silent for a moment, still reading. "Kind of nerve-racking, isn't it? The CIA had him for a month before they sent him up here. Never flagged up anything wrong with him. Yikes. Bet they're feeling pretty pie-faced now."

"I bet," I said, looking at the photograph and his dimpled, grinning face.

Jo leaned forward to take a look for herself.

"Well, somebody's getting sacked," she said. "Letting a Red agent get that close to the president. Letting them shake hands."

"I'm sure they searched him first."

"That's the thing. They wouldn't have found a weapon. I was actually reading about this in the *Post*—the *Saturday Evening Post*. They did a piece on this guy, this defector, who had been a Red assassin in Berlin—it was called 'I Would Not Murder for the Soviets.' He was talking about how he had poison bullets in this little gun shaped like a cigarette case—and they had photos of the gun, and it really did just look like a cigarette case. He just had to pretend he was going for a cigarette, and—*bang*."

"Well, he didn't," I said. "Maksym, I mean. He didn't do anything."

"It's the idea that he could have," Jo said. "He could have, and they couldn't have stopped him. That's the scary part."

She had to leave at six o'clock to go to a ladies' auxiliary meeting. The technicians finished up and tramped out a few minutes later. I sat at the kitchen table and dialed Dad's office number. I assumed because it was his direct line he would be the only one to pick up, but instead I got somebody named

Lieutenant Weller, who told me, over the insistent clacking of typewriter keys in the background, that Colonel Blaine wasn't in.

"You mean not on base?"

A pause. More clacking. "Who did you say this was?"

"His daughter. Shelby Blaine. He told me to call."

"His daughter," Lieutenant Weller informed somebody else, muffling the speaker rather ineffectually. The typewriter keys continued unabated.

"Here, send her over," somebody else said.

I heard the stiff, electric crackle as the call was transferred to another line.

"He can't take a call right now," the voice at the other end said. "Need something?"

It was an oddly familiar voice, but I couldn't place it. "Who is this?"

"This is Agent Jones."

And then I could picture him in my head—cool-eyed and scowling, twirling his toothpick. My stomach turned over uneasily. I didn't have any rationale left for distrusting him; whatever doubts and suspicions Dad might have had about him seemed dispelled by the fact that he was the one who had put the actual Red agent out of commission. But Dad had not only distrusted but disliked him, and while I supposed Dad could occasionally get his facts wrong like any of the rest of us, he was very rarely wrong in his judgments of people's character.

"I'll just call back," I said.

"Hang on," Agent Jones said.

"What?"

"I said hang on for a second. Why'd he want you to call?"

"What?" I repeated stupidly.

"You said he told you to call."

And all I had to say was, "Oh, he wanted me to let him know the phone company got our line hooked up"—just like that. But instead what came out of my mouth was "I don't see that it's any of your business."

"Given the circumstances, Miss Blaine," he said, "it is, in fact, my business."

That *Miss Blaine* touched off a fuse.

"I must have misunderstood, Agent Jones. I thought your business was making sure the Red spy didn't get away in the first place."

A stretch of tinny telephone silence followed—long enough for the fuse to sputter. I wished I could take it back. What a stupid, stupid thing to say. This man could end Dad's career with one word. He could make sure I never got into Bryn Mawr.

Another crackle of static. "Sorry—what was that, Miss Blaine?"

He hadn't even been listening.

"*Arschloch*," I snapped, and slammed the receiver back onto the cradle.

My head was pounding. I wasn't sure whether it was nerves or sheer fury. I took two aspirin tablets from the bottle in my handbag and went to run a bath.

I was completely undressed and just about done filling the tub before I remembered I had left my towel draped over my closet door yesterday. I slipped my sundress back on—old habit from living in base housing at Ramstein; you never took a chance with the windows open—and darted barefoot out into the hall.

I smacked face-first into something warm and solid.

The thing let out a winded grunt, alarmingly human, and I screamed. A callused hand clamped tightly over my mouth. I tasted blood and salt.

"*Shhh*—please. It's okay," Maksym said.

SIX

I CLAWED HIS HAND AWAY, pummeled him wildly with both fists, and stumbled for the telephone in the kitchen, spitting his blood and scrubbing it from my lips with the back of my hand.

"Wait," he said, limping after me, dragging his right foot with effort. His voice was thick. "Please, Shelby—it's okay. Please don't telephone. Please."

"Get away from me," I snarled, and he froze there in the kitchen doorway, holding up his hands as though in surrender.

I had no idea how he could be on his feet. His right ankle was clearly broken. His trousers were torn from hem to knee, and the ankle was swollen like a lump of yeast dough let to stand too long. He was a mess of sweat and dirt and bruises and blood. His lips were split. A wide, purpling bruise mottled his left cheek from the corner of his mouth to his eye socket. His hands were scored all over with deep scratches and gouges as if he had tried, unsuccessfully, to fend off a very large and very ferocious cat.

But I wasn't stupid. He still had the advantage. He wasn't big, but he was solid muscle. He hadn't even seemed to notice that I was hitting him.

My hands wouldn't cooperate. I held the telephone receiver to my ear, fumbling at the dial with numb, slippery fingers. The scrap of paper with Dad's office number went fluttering gently to the floor, coming to rest right at Maksym's feet.

He crouched very slowly to pick it up.

"Give it to me." I was clutching the receiver so tightly that my hand was shaking.

He straightened, leaning a shoulder carefully on the doorjamb, shifting his weight off his foot. He kept one mangled hand up, palm toward me, but he tucked the other inside the breast of his coat.

"Listen first," he challenged.

"Give me that paper. Put it on the table."

He withdrew a pistol from his coat, lifted his arm, and trained the pistol on my face.

"Please, Shelby," he said softly. "Listen."

I stood there staring into the muzzle of that pistol, the receiver clamped uselessly against my ear. *He disarmed an MP*, Agent Kimball said, *disarmed him, knocked him out*—and I had heard every word and understood every word, and still somehow it had not sunk in until this moment that he would be carrying a gun.

I couldn't tell you what sort of pistol it was. My only experience with pistols was when Uncle Fred let me shoot his Sport-King once on the farm in Ohio, when I was fourteen or so and we were stateside on leave. But I knew that unwieldy, pipelike thing screwed onto the barrel was a silencer. Nobody was going to hear a shot from that pistol. Jo's was the closest house, and it was nearly a ten minute walk away.

I had to keep him talking. I could dial the central office behind my back if I was careful.

I squared my shoulders. "Fine. Talk."

"It's a mistake. Only a mistake."

"Then explain to them."

"I can't explain to them. The photos—it's a mistake. But I can't explain to them."

I edged in against the table, trying to put the telephone cradle out of his line of sight. "What photos?"

"They took photos. Danish intelligence at Bornholm. They took photos of my plane after the crash to give to CIA. Because it was, um . . ." He struggled for a moment, searching for the word. His accent was thicker now than it had been last night. He was exhausted—or last night had been an act he simply wasn't bothering to put on today. "Prototype. Prototype plane. Top secret, okay? They want photos. CIA. Air Force."

I searched across the cradle with my fingertips. "So what's the mistake?"

"Because they think I'm lying," he said wearily. "They think I'm lying when I tell them I was shot down. They think I'm lying when I tell them I want to defect. They think I sabotaged the plane myself. They have photos of the cockpit—the controls. The damage from the shooting. Colonel Blaine says autocannon doesn't do that. Autocannon doesn't damage inside the cockpit like that. He says I set a bomb to sabotage the plane. But it wasn't a bomb. Zhenya—my wingman—he hit the fuel line. He was shooting when I ejected, and one of the rounds hit the fuel line." He closed his free hand in a fist, then uncurled his fingers all at once, mimicking an explosion—*boom*. "No bomb."

"Then tell them that."

"I tried to tell them that."

"Everything you just told me. Everything you just said about the fuel line."

"Yeah. I tried to tell them. They don't believe me. They think I'm a spy—all of them. Jones, Colonel Blaine, all of them. But I'm not a spy."

I hesitated, forefinger on the dial. Of course they didn't believe him. They hadn't trusted him to begin with. He had switched sides; he was a traitor. *Nobody trusts a traitor.*

His gaze hung on me warily. I had the feeling he knew exactly what I was doing behind my back.

"Please," he said. "Please don't telephone."

Even if I managed to get through to the central office before he pulled that trigger, he would be gone by the time the police got here.

He would be gone, and I would be dead. He was desperate and afraid, I could hear it in his voice, but his hand was steady, practiced; the pistol hadn't wavered once. His face was set like stone. He knew what he was doing.

It was a little past six. Dad would be home soon. I just needed to keep doing what I was doing—keep him talking, keep him calm.

I drew a careful breath, trying to compose myself—trying very hard not to think about the fact that I wasn't wearing a stitch beneath the thin cotton seersucker of my sundress, and he could almost certainly tell. Thank God, *thank God* I had bothered to throw the dress on. I hadn't bothered to zip it up the back.

I said, "Maybe you should tell me what you're doing here."

His shoulders loosened a little, though he didn't lower the pistol. "I was looking for . . . tape? A tape."

"What kind of tape?"

"For this. For the ankle." He made an awkward, grimacing gesture at his right foot. "I saw you leave—in the red car with your friend. I was out there in the woods, hiding in the woods. I saw you leave. And I needed the tape for the ankle, and the house was empty, so—"

"I locked the doors. I always lock the doors."

"Yeah," he said, with a kind of half shame, half triumph—as though he'd come across the answer key for the math test in the teacher's desk. "You use a shim to open the lock. It's called a shim. Jones showed me how to do it—to open handcuffs. You have a little piece of metal, like the, um—the clip from a pen, okay—"

"Well, we don't have any tape," I said curtly. Why on earth had Agent Jones taught him how to escape handcuffs?

"Yeah. No tape. I found out."

"So why are you still here?"

"I was hiding." Another awkward gesture, this time toward the linen closet at the end of the hall. "Colonel Blaine came with FBI, so I was hiding—there."

"This whole time." I felt a little unsteady on my feet. This whole time—while Jo and I were sitting there reading the paper, while the technicians were putting in the phone . . .

"This whole time—yeah. Then I heard the bath, and I thought—"

The bath.

I slammed the telephone receiver down, unthinking, and he gave a start. I had left the bathwater running.

Somebody chose that moment to knock on the door.

For half a second, Maksym and I stood frozen, looking at each other. Jo was at a ladies' auxiliary meeting. Dad wouldn't knock.

The knock was repeated. "Hello! Miss Blaine?"—an unfamiliar man's voice. "Miss Blaine, this is Sergeant Riley, police."

My stomach lurched. Maksym stood absolutely still, watching me.

"Hello—Miss Blaine?"

I shut my eyes.

"*Scheisse*," I said, "*Scheisse, Scheisse*"—and then, to Maksym, opening my eyes: "Go turn the water off."

"What?"

"The bathwater," I said calmly, though my insides were in knots—oh God, I couldn't let him shoot a cop. "Go turn the bathwater off. Stay there. Be quiet."

"Don't answer the door."

"I have to answer it."

"Shelby." He made a quick, taut motion with the pistol.

"I have to answer it. Dad must have sent him. If I don't answer the door, he's going to think something is wrong."

He hesitated.

Another knock, insistent now. "Miss Blaine? Police. Open up."

Maksym exhaled heavily through his nostrils, defeated and frustrated. His mouth was set in a grim, tight line.

"Okay—come," he said.

"What?"

"Come." He beckoned sharply with the pistol. "Answer it."

He herded me to the door with the muzzle of the pistol leveled directly at the side of my head. He positioned himself just behind me, holding on to my left arm with his free hand—not roughly but firmly, his fingers pressed tight around my elbow. I didn't dare try to pull away or shove him off. I could feel the tremors of tension fluttering in his fingers; I could hear the soft hitch in his breath. All it would take was one nervous spasm of his trigger finger, and—

Keep him calm. Keep him calm.

"Maksym." My heart was in my mouth. "Maksym—you've got to let go of my arm."

And he did.

He didn't drop the pistol away from my head, but he let go of my elbow all at once, as if he hadn't realized he was holding it.

I swallowed my heart back down, zipped up my dress like a suit of armor, smoothed my hair and straightened my shoulders, and opened the door.

"Hello—I'm sorry. I was taking a telephone call."

Sergeant Riley touched his cap to me but didn't take it off. "Miss Blaine," he said. He was a mountain of a man; I had to take a step back to look him in the face. He was scowling behind his neatly trimmed mustache. He had a thumb hooked on the grip of the pistol holstered at his hip.

"Just wanted to give you the courtesy, ma'am," he said. "Wanted to let you know we're going to be patrolling the area. Didn't want you to be alarmed when you saw the cruiser on the street."

I leaned on the door. I could feel Maksym there behind me—I could feel the pistol leveled at my temple—and it took concentrated effort not to give him away by turning my head or flicking a glance at him sidelong. "Does that mean you haven't found him? The Russian?"

"Not yet—no, ma'am. But we'll get him, don't worry."

Sergeant Riley shifted his weight from booted foot to booted foot. I thought he was turning to go, but instead he stood there giving me an unsubtle once-over, head to toe and back up to my face.

I moved a little to the side, putting the door between us, which seemed to embarrass him a bit.

"Sorry, ma'am, but are you all right?"

"Excuse me?"

"You're bleeding," he said.

My hand flew reflexively to my mouth. I felt across my lips with the backs of my fingers. Sergeant Riley said, scowling, "No—there. Your arm. Are you hurt?"

I twisted my arm around to look. There was a complete set of fingerprints in bloody smears above my elbow. One of Maksym's hands must have caught me there when I ran into him in the hall. The prints were on the back of my arm. Neither of us had noticed.

"Oh, this—an accident. Just an accident." I managed a smile. It felt obviously phony—too stiff, too wide. My jaw ached. "I—I was picking up some broken glass. I think I must have cut my hand."

Sergeant Riley threw a glance around the living room behind me, then gave me a slow, skeptical nod. "Well, I'll be around if you need me."

"Thank you," I said, smiling at him.

He touched his cap again and stalked off down the driveway to his car. I shut the door and stood there for a moment, resting my forehead on the cool veneered wood, listening to the car door slam and the engine turn over—listening to him drive off and leave me.

I felt the whisper of movement as Maksym took the pistol away from my temple. I lifted my head. His brow was knitted in that little scowl. He was trying to get a look at my arm.

"I hurt you?" he asked.

I brushed the blood off with a swipe of my hand, deliberately keeping the arm away from him. It was the most defiance I could muster.

"I have to turn the bath off," I said.

The hall bathroom was swimming. Water cascaded in graceful sheets down the side of the tub, flooding across the floor tiles, soaking through my discarded shoes and clothes and under the baseboards and into the hall carpet. I splashed through on tiptoes, shut off the tap, and reached in to pull the drain plug. Maksym had come limping along behind me, and now he stood hovering uncertainly in the doorway, pistol in hand, watching me gather up my dripping underthings and drape them over the side of the tub.

"Enjoying the show?" I snarled.

He looked quickly away, pretending he hadn't been watching. He had the decency to flush a little. I pushed past him out into the hall.

"Look—stand here. You can watch me all the way to the kitchen, see? I'm going to get the mop."

He was in the bathroom when I came back. He was making a futile attempt to wipe water off the floor with the hand towel. He leaned on the counter, pushing the towel slowly and carefully with his good foot. The pistol was nowhere in sight. He wasn't looking up, and he must not have heard my footsteps over the sound of the draining tub. He gave a little start when he caught sight of me in the doorway.

"Listen to me." I was calmer now that I had something to hold on to—something to do with my hands. I was gripping the mop like a weapon. "You can shoot me if you want, but you heard Sergeant Riley. They're patrolling the streets. They're going to see you if you try to leave—and even if they don't catch you, they're going to radio it in to base, and Agent Jones is going to come for you, and Agent Kimball, and everybody. You're not going to get away."

He was silent for a moment, then he ducked his head and went back to pushing the towel with his foot.

"I don't want to shoot you," he said.

"Listen. I'm trying to give you a fair shake. You can wait for Dad. You can explain to him."

He let out a soft breath. "Colonel Blaine doesn't believe me. I already told you."

"Nobody's going to believe you if you shoot me. And that's your only other option. I could telephone Agent Jones as soon as you're out the door." I swallowed. "If you want them to believe you, you've got to stop running."

He was silent, pushing the towel, close-cut head bent. His brow was wrinkled in that scowl again, like a neat little chevron notched between his eyebrows.

I swooped to snatch the sopping towel away from him. "Stop doing that. It's not doing anything. You're just moving the water around."

"Why do you say it?" he asked. "*Scheisse.*"

"What?"

"In the kitchen you said *Scheisse.*"

I slung the towel over the side of the tub. This, of all the things he could possibly have latched on to? "It's German. It means . . . you're frustrated. It's what you say when you're frustrated."

"Yeah," he said, "I know what it is." There was a tremor in his voice. I recognized carefully contained anger. "Why do you speak German?"

I paused midstep, leaning on the mop. Broken ankle, face and hands in shreds—but that word was what hurt him.

He was Ukrainian; he was a Soviet citizen. He had lived under the German occupation. The war had been real for him in a way it had never been for me, even with Dad gone and Mom working full-time at the aircraft plant in Columbus. I knew the casualty numbers because we learned them in school: more than twenty million Soviet dead. He hadn't had to learn the cost of the war from a textbook.

"We lived there," I said quietly. "Dad was stationed there—West Germany. We were there for seven years. We just moved back this week."

"Ramstein?"

"Yes."

He was standing stock-still. His face was shuttered tight, deliberately blank. He wasn't really much taller than I was, just a few finger widths, except he was wearing shoes and I was barefoot. But he seemed taller all at once, more imposing—dangerous and unpredictable, like a revolver with one round somewhere in the cylinder.

I was suddenly conscious of how small this space was, how close I was to him. Never mind that pistol—he could close the distance between us in one step and have his hands on me.

"It's just a habit," I said. "I'm sorry."

I wasn't sure at first that he had heard me. He wasn't really looking at me. He was looking at some indefinite point above my right ear, his eyes far away and thoughtful. But then he nodded once, slowly, as if he had weighed this and accepted it.

"It's okay," he said. He brushed a glance over me. "This . . . ," he said, touching his right elbow with his fingers. "I hurt you?"

"You didn't hurt me."

We stood there looking at each other uncertainly, as if a cease-fire had just been declared and we were each looking to see who was going to put down their weapons first.

"What happened to you anyway?" I asked. "Your hands, your face . . ."

He looked down at his scratched, bleeding hands as if they were a sudden revelation—as if he hadn't noticed until now. Maybe he hadn't. "I climbed over a fence at the base. Barbed wire fence."

"Well, the fence wins that round. Who socked you one? Agent Jones?"

"Socked me one?"

"Your face. Who hit you?"

He touched his battered cheek reflexively. "Yeah—Jones. Because they said I will go to Moscow for the prisoner exchange. I tried to fight, and he . . ." He paused, testing the new expression carefully. "Socked me one."

"Let me take care of this, and I'll patch you up," I said.

"Okay," he said.

And I already knew the answer, but I asked him anyway because I wanted him to know I understood.

"Did you lose anybody?" I asked. "In the war?"

Another slow, careful nod. He was still looking at his hands.

"Everybody," he said.

SEVEN

I WENT AROUND AND CLOSED all the window blinds and switched on the kitchen light. The sun had slipped behind the trees. It was getting dark on the street now, and you could see right into our living room through the big window beside the door. Maksym was on the sofa with his shoes off, his right foot propped up on the coffee table, his shoulders slumped into the cushions, head tipped back. He wasn't saying anything, just staring at the ceiling as though he were trying to read some message hidden in the stucco finish, but I could tell he was hurting. I brought him a couple of aspirin tablets from my handbag, a glass of water, and handfuls of ice cubes knotted in kitchen towels for his face and ankle, and he turned his head against the cushions and offered me that dimpled grin, shyer and more tentative now that we had seen each other on war footing.

Oh God—that grin was going to kill me.

I sat beside him on the edge of the sofa, my housecoat pulled securely tight around me, and took his hands across my lap one after the other so I could wrap them with strips cut and knotted together from another kitchen towel. I didn't have proper bandages, and I didn't have wound ointment or antiseptic.

He needed antiseptic. I was honestly more worried about his hands than about his broken ankle. Anything about barbed wire cuts made me nervous. Uncle Fred, Dad's older brother who kept up the family dairy farm outside Columbus, could tell you horror stories about rusty wire and tetanus amputations. It was one of those childhood fears that had stayed with me while all the rest—quicksand, volcanic eruptions, the Black Death—receded into the flat, boring Ohio distance as I got older.

I kept my head intently down as I worked. I didn't trust myself to look up into his face. His hands were like Dad's, tanned and rough-skinned—farmer's hands, laborer's hands. It made me wonder whether he had always meant to be a pilot or whether he, like Dad, had been just some farm boy who stumbled into flying mostly by accident—whether there could even be accidents like that in Russia or whether everything was always according to plan, the party's plan. I supposed at some point the plan had gone wrong or he wouldn't be sitting here in my living room.

There were scars here and there on his tanned skin—old wounds beneath the new ones. Most of them were the ordinary little nicks and furrows you would expect on hands like his, but there was a long, pale old scar on the outside of his left forearm that made my breath catch. It had been deep, this cut, and it had been deliberate. It was too surgically neat to have been an accident.

I paused too long, holding his forearm under my fingers and looking at that scar, and he raised his head to look. I felt him twitch a little, a tremor running down his arm, as if he were squeamish about letting me touch it. I let go of his arm and went back to wrapping his palm.

"That one looks like it hurt," I said.

He dropped his head back against the cushions. "Yeah. It's okay now."

"How did it happen?"

"In the war," he said. "When does Colonel Blaine come?"

I tied off the strip of towel, and he cradled his arm close against his stomach and pulled his coat sleeve down carefully over the scar, hiding it away again. I looked away. I wished I hadn't asked. It was stupid of me—thinking we understood each other because I had lost somebody. He had the war carved into his body.

"He said he'd be back at six thirty," I said, "maybe seven."

Maksym looked at his wristwatch. I looked at mine. It was ten past seven.

"Something must have come up," I muttered.

"They must not have found that Russian yet," he said.

We sat in silence; we were both on edge. It was ghastly hot in the house with the blinds closed, no breeze. Maksym's ice packs melted. I wrung out the towels and brought him more. I couldn't tell whether he honestly believed me—whether he honestly thought he had a chance to get Dad to believe him if they could just talk airman to airman, away from the stifling formality of the debriefing room and the presence of Agent Jones—or whether the ankle was hurting too badly now for him to care one way or another. Even under ice, it was swollen like a puff pastry and starting to turn black.

He fell asleep.

I could see him start to slip, his shoulders loosening, and I sat very still while his eyelids drifted slowly shut. His head dropped to the side, his cheek settling against the wadded towel. His breath hitched and then started again, long and low and steady.

His suit coat gaped open. The burnished wood of the pistol grip peeked from his lining pocket.

I had to take it now. I wouldn't have a better chance. I didn't want him to have that gun when Dad walked through the door.

Scarcely daring to breathe, I leaned over him, reaching across his chest with shaking fingers.

The telephone rang.

I jumped. He started violently beneath me, his eyelids flying open.

"Your ice pack," I said stupidly. My voice was hoarse; my throat was closed. "It melted again. I was going to bring you another one."

He blinked up at me. He wasn't quite awake yet.

"Okay," he said.

I took the dripping towel and escaped into the kitchen.

"Blaine household," I said, balancing the receiver between my cheek and shoulder while I twisted out the towel in the sink. My hands were shaking.

"Hi, Shel," Dad said.

"Hi." I leaned on the counter. The kitchen door was open. Maksym was watching me over his shoulder from the sofa. I couldn't tell whether he had the pistol out again. "I tried to call."

"Yeah," he said, "yeah, I know. Jones said you called. Gave me the number."

I hadn't given Agent Jones the number, which meant he had called the central office and asked for it. I supposed that was my fault; it had been incredibly stupid to curse him out and hang up on him—but still. One more item to add to the list of things that irked me about Agent Jones, right after his idiotic toothpick and his *Given the circumstances, Miss Blaine*—and the marks of his fist on Maksym's face, if I was being completely honest. Maksym had been unarmed at that point, certainly outnumbered. Surely there had been a way to incapacitate him without slugging him across the face.

"Yeah," I said lightly. "He said you were busy."

"Look, I'm sorry, Shel, it's just been—a mess, really. A hell of a mess. That's the only way to put it. We've got four, five, six different agencies here—and somebody from the NSC— all trying to run the show the way they think it should run and to hell with everybody else, and nobody's actually got a damn clue. It's a hell of a mess."

"Are you still on base?"

"Yeah, still on base. Listen—sorry I didn't call sooner. I thought I was going to be able to get away for a bit."

"It's okay."

"I did remember about dinner," he said. "I know we were supposed to go out."

"It's okay."

"Did you eat?"

I hadn't once thought about eating. My stomach was a solid, bristling lump of nerves. "Not yet."

"You've got something to eat?"

"Yes—I just . . . if you were going to be home, I didn't want to—"

"Don't wait for me," he said. "Go ahead and eat. Don't wait for me."

"Okay," I managed.

"Listen, Shel," he said, "I'm going to stay over on base

tonight, okay? I think that'll be easiest. Won't have to wake you up coming in or anything. It's going to be a late night, probably an early morning. Is that okay?"

I opened my mouth, then closed it. Panic fluttered like a moth in my throat.

"Shel?" Dad asked. "Shel, did you hear me?"

"Yes." It spilled out automatically. "Yes, that's okay. That's fine."

"Is the car there?"

"The car?"

"City police said they were going to send a patrol car up there."

"Oh—yes. Yes, he's here. Sergeant Riley. He's been here since about six or so. He said they'll be patrolling."

"Good," Dad said, "good. Listen, call this number if you need something, okay? The office number. If you need anything. And—Shel? Do me a favor. Lock the door, will you? The front door. It was open this afternoon—when Kimball and I got there. I don't want you leaving the doors open anymore. Even in the daytime, okay? Even if you're home. Do me a favor and lock them."

"Yes," I said, heart thudding in my ears, "yes, okay."

"All right," he said. "I love you."

"Hey, Dad . . . ," I started.

"Yeah?"

I wound the phone cord around one trembling finger after another. I could just see the top of Maksym's close-cut scalp over the back of the sofa. His head had dropped to his shoulder again.

He had fallen back asleep.

And I couldn't do it. I couldn't make myself do it.

There was simply no way he was a Red agent.

He could have just shot me. A Red agent would have. A Red agent wouldn't have any qualms about it—not if I were putting his mission in jeopardy. He wouldn't have stood there in my kitchen trying to explain himself to me. He wouldn't have wasted the precious time.

A Red agent wouldn't let himself fall asleep on my sofa.

Oh God—I was just Shelby Blaine. I shouldn't have anything to do with any of this. I shouldn't even be here. I should be on my way to Columbus to put my mother's ashes in the ground, and Maksym Ivanovych Whatever-His-Name-Was should be nothing more than a mildly thrilling anecdote for me to pull out and dust off at dinner parties—*that time there was a Russian spy hiding in my linen closet.*

We weren't leaving for Columbus tonight. I could let him sleep for a few more hours. One small kindness—probably the last he was going to get.

"Nothing," I said into the phone. "I love you."

"I love you too," Dad said. "I'll see you tomorrow, okay?"

"Okay," I said.

EIGHT

I FELL ASLEEP AT THE kitchen table.

I didn't mean to. I made myself a cup of Nescafé and settled in at the table with the intention of spending a sleepless night positioned very strategically between Maksym and the front door, with a clear line of sight to the carport door and within arm's reach of the telephone—and the next thing I knew, I was waking up slowly and groggily under the harsh fluorescent glare of the overhead light, my face buried in my arms, *Homage to Catalonia* spread open under my cheek. Somebody was fumbling at the front door lock.

It was dark and silent in the living room. How long had I been asleep? The hands of my watch said 7:36, but that didn't make any sense, because it had been almost eight o'clock when I talked to Dad—

I sat straight up, heart lurching. It was 7:36 in the morning. It was dark in the living room because I had closed all the blinds last night.

Dad swung the door open. Bright, bright morning sunlight flooded in, sweeping across the living room like a searchlight.

Maksym was gone.

"Hey, Shel," Dad said from the doorway, then paused. "Did you sleep out here?"

I nearly tripped over the hem of my housecoat trying to get out of that kitchen chair. The sofa was empty, the cushions carefully straightened and plumped. His shoes were gone; the dish towels were gone; the water glass I had brought him was gone. He must have woken up at some point in the night. He must have taken a chance on the police patrols and slipped out into the dark without waking me.

He was gone. You couldn't tell he had ever been here.

Scheisse, I thought—and then felt guilty for thinking it, and an inexplicable little ache blossomed under my ribs.

"I guess I did," I said. "I was reading. I guess I just fell asleep."

Dad shut the door and tossed his cap onto the kitchen counter. He looked ashy-faced and tired. The hollows and lines in his face were deep and dark. A scattering of silver-gray stubble had sprung up on his jaw. I doubted he had gotten a wink of sleep last night.

"Well, sorry to wake you up," he said. "Thought you'd be up. I guess seven thirty's pretty early for the summer, isn't it?"

My hands shook a little as I brought out the coffee jar from under the counter. I felt as if it were printed across my face in big, front-page headline letters: *He was here! I helped him hide! I could have turned him in, but I didn't!* It felt impossible that Dad couldn't tell just by looking at me.

"Did they find him?" I asked. "The Russian?" They must have found him. He didn't have a chance on that ankle—not in daylight, not with the police patrolling Birchwood and six different agencies looking for him.

And if they had found him, and if he had told them where he had been all yesterday afternoon . . .

"Not yet," Dad said. "Kimball says they've got some leads." He shrugged off his jacket as he went into the hall. "Going to hop in the shower," he said. "I've got twenty minutes before I'm supposed to be briefing that NSC guy."

"Time for coffee?"

He threw me a quick smile over his shoulder. "Coffee would be good."

I put the kettle on and measured the grounds into two cups. This was a hell of a mess, all right. They were going to find Maksym sooner or later, and he was going to spill where he had been, and it was going to look pretty suspicious if I hadn't said anything. I could explain away why I hadn't given him up to Sergeant Riley or to Dad over the phone; he had threatened me with a gun to my head, after all. But I didn't have any reason to keep mum now, with him out of the house.

I twisted the lid back onto the Nescafé jar grimly. I couldn't tell them he had threatened me. If I told them that, he wouldn't ever make it to Moscow for a prisoner exchange. Dad would kill him himself.

And what was the use, really, of either of us trying to explain that he was innocent? They weren't going to believe me any more than they had believed Maksym himself in the debriefing room. I was nice little blond Miss Blaine, typical female who didn't know any better, and he was That Russian— the traitor, the guy who had switched sides once and could do it again. They were never going to believe he was innocent; they were certainly never going to believe it from me. They would just think I had gone weak at the knees for that grin and those honey-brown eyes and the soft way he had said, "Please, Shelby," when he held that pistol on me.

So now I was nice little blond Miss Blaine who had harbored a federal fugitive, no excuses.

Harboring a fugitive wasn't the same as spying. It wasn't treason. I would probably only get jail time, not the electric chair. But then, they had executed Ethel Rosenberg two summers ago, and she wasn't technically a spy either, just the one who typed up the papers—an "accessory." I would be the accessory in an espionage case against Maksym—and harboring a fugitive was a lot worse than typing up papers.

Maybe they wouldn't find him.

"What kind of leads?" I asked Dad when he came back into the kitchen.

"What?" He was fastening his wristwatch. His tie hung loose around his neck. I caught a whiff of his Lenthéric Tanbark after-shave lotion—sharp spice and wood and leather. I had always loved that smell. It was comforting because it was constant. There were very few constants in this sort of life, the Air Force life. Dad's Tanbark was one of the few. Mom had given him a set every Christmas.

"You said Agent Kimball said they've got some leads."

"Says he's got some leads over in Syracuse," Dad said distractedly, finishing his wristwatch and starting on his tie.

"Syracuse?"

"About forty-five miles west of here." He added for my benefit, tugging at his tie, "Seventy kilometers or so."

Maksym couldn't have made seventy kilometers in one

night—not on foot, not on that ankle. Even if he had left Rome yesterday afternoon, the way Agent Kimball supposed, he couldn't have made seventy kilometers. "Why Syracuse?"

"There's a pretty big immigrant population in Syracuse— Ukrainians, Poles. Ex-Soviet émigrés. Kimball thinks he'll surface there—thinks he may have had a prearranged contact there."

I threaded my fingers together around my cup and looked at my own reflection scattered on the surface of the coffee. I didn't want him seeing anything in my face. "Assuming he really is a spy."

Dad gave his tie one last tug and reached for his coffee cup. "We combed every inch of the base grounds," he said. "Didn't find a trace of him. No footprints, no tracks."

It was sort of like looking at somebody else's math problem set, trying to catch up with the way Dad's mind worked— somebody much better than you at math. You couldn't always see how he got to the answer because he moved so quickly and never bothered showing his work, the steps were so obvious to him. "So?"

"Means he knows what he's doing," Dad said. "Or it means he's got help."

He downed his Nescafé in three quick swallows and reached for his cap. I just barely felt him lean in to kiss my cheek, smelling of coffee and Tanbark.

"Keep the doors locked," he said.

A CAR WENT BY ON the street while I was rinsing out the coffee cups and turning them upside down on the counter to dry. I heard the low mutter of the engine. I leaned on my tiptoes over the sink, separated the slats of the window blind with a fingertip, and watched a City of Rome patrol car trundle down toward the unfinished end of the cul-de-sac, swing around at the edge of the pavement, and go slowly back the way it had come.

And I knew they were just patrolling, the way Sergeant Riley had told me they would, and I knew they were keeping an eye on this cul-de-sac in particular because it was the one that ran nearest the woods and the river, but it still made me uneasy. I had the sick, guilty feeling that they were watching the house.

He's got help, Dad said.

Could he know? Maybe he had been trying to drop a hint. Maybe the police had started to suspect that Maksym might have come here. Birchwood was the first housing development you came to once you left base, and there were only so many houses in Birchwood.

But of course that didn't make any sense. If Dad thought I was helping Maksym, he wouldn't just drop some vague hint about it on his way out the door. If the police thought Maksym was here, they wouldn't just be leisurely cruising the cul-de-sac.

I let go of the slats and dropped back onto my heels. It was all a moot point anyway. He wasn't here anymore.

"Good morning," he said.

I whirled, nearly sending the cups to the floor.

He was there in the doorway, leaning his shoulder on the jamb, keeping his weight off his swollen foot. He had one Oxford shoe on—the left. He carried the right in his hand. He hadn't been able to get that one on over the swelling.

I found the edge of the counter behind me and leaned on

it, trying not to show him how much he had startled me. "I thought you were gone."

"No, only hiding. I heard the car—Colonel Blaine's car." He gestured with the shoe to illustrate, holding on to the doorjamb with his free hand. He looked tired; he sounded tired. His face was drawn and pale beneath the bruises. "You didn't tell him."

"What?"

"You didn't tell him I was here."

I said, "I thought you were gone. It didn't matter."

"No. On the telephone. Last night."

I opened my mouth—he had been asleep; how could he possibly know?—and closed it again. He would have known, of course, when he woke up this morning still here, still free.

He ran a glance over my face as though searching for something; then he let go of the doorjamb to fumble at his coat lining.

"I have this—for the trouble, to say thank you—"

"What are you doing?"

"Going now, before they find me here." He was digging in his lining pocket, brushing the pistol aside. "They will know you didn't tell Colonel Blaine. They will know you helped me."

"Wait."

"Yesterday you could have told them it was only because of this"—he indicated the pistol—"because I would shoot you if you didn't help me—"

"*Wait*," I snapped, and he froze.

I dug thumb and forefinger into my eyelids. "There's a patrol car out there. You can't just walk out the door."

"They aren't watching the house," he said. "They're watching the trees. It's okay."

"You can't even get your shoes on. You can't even stand up straight."

He looked at the shoe in his hand, then critically at his swollen foot, straightening against the doorjamb as if to prove he could. "It doesn't hurt. It looks bad but doesn't hurt. Maybe not a break. Only . . . sprain. Not a break."

"Listen to me. If they catch you, they're going to ask where you were. You're going to have to tell them where you were."

"I won't tell them," he said quietly. "It's okay."

"Stop saying 'it's okay' and *listen* to me. They'll figure it out. They think you're seventy kilometers away in some place called Syracuse. If they pick you up here in Rome, if they find out you've been in Rome this whole time, they're going to know somebody must have been hiding you—helping you. And then they're going to know you're lying to them. Again."

"Not a lie," he said. "The photos—a mistake. Only a mistake."

"Why didn't they find your footprints?"

He looked at me quickly, that questioning little V notched between his brows.

"At the base," I said. "They never found any footprints. They never found any tracks. Do you know what that makes them think?"

He gave one slow shake of his head.

"It makes them think you've had training."

"Training?"

"It makes them think you're a spy."

"I'm not a spy," he said.

"All right, so why didn't they find any footprints?"

He looked honestly bewildered, as if he couldn't believe

he had to explain this to me. "I walked on the pavement. On the pavement, then in the—um . . ." I could practically see him searching around in his head for the words. He dipped the shoe in his hand, trying to illustrate. "To take the water to the canal."

"Culvert. Ditch—drainage ditch?"

"Drainage ditch," he echoed a little uncertainly. "With the little rocks."

"Gravel?"

"Gravel, yeah. No footprints."

"That's what they mean. You break an ankle jumping from a second-story window, and you still have the presence of mind to say, 'Okay, better walk in a drainage ditch so I don't leave any footprints.'"

The puzzled furrow deepened. "I don't want them to find me. So I walk in a place where I don't leave footprints."

"Well, that's what makes them think you've had training."

"It's what we did during the war," he said. "It's not training, only being careful. We used the river so we didn't leave footprints for Germans to find. Or Russians. We fought both of them." A sharp note crept into his voice—a sudden, impatient lashing of anger. "Why do they think I spy for the Russians? I hate the Russians."

"You flew planes for them."

"Because I have to escape. I'm not KGB. I'm not a politician or . . . diplomat, with a chance to travel. My only chance is to fly planes. So I fly planes."

He was worked up now, and he had that pistol. I wasn't afraid of him; I knew he wasn't really angry at me. But I was afraid he was going to turn on his heel, his one good heel, and march right out the door in a flash of stupid defiance. I shouldn't have jabbed him about the planes.

"Maksym," I said softly, "if you walk out that door, they're going to catch you. And it's both our necks if they catch you anywhere near here. We've got to be smart about this. We've got to think."

I had him pinned, and he knew it. He looked away. His mouth was set in that stubborn, tight line, but he nodded once.

"Would you like some eggs?" I asked.

He looked back, head tilted, as though he wasn't sure he had heard me right.

"I'm starving. I know you have to be." I opened the refrigerator. I didn't really feel any hungrier now than I had felt last night; my nerves were too jangled. But I needed the comfort of doing something absolutely mundane. "When's the last time you ate?"

His hollow gaze followed my hand to the egg carton. He swallowed. I could see him fighting with himself. Slowly, very slowly, he shook his head.

"No, thank you," he said.

"Well, you can't lie worth beans, can you?" I took four eggs from the carton.

"Worth beans?"

"It means you don't lie very well."

"I don't lie," he said stiffly. "Only a mistake. Not a lie."

"Relax. It was a joke," I said.

He drew something from his lining pocket and held it out to me, hand shaking a little.

I just about dropped the eggs. Hundred-dollar bills—multiple hundred-dollar bills.

He must have had three hundred dollars in his hand. He was offering it to me.

My voice stumbled out in a whisper. "What is that?"

"For you. I want to pay."

"What?"

He paused, considered, seemed to come to a realization. He amended his wording.

"For the eggs," he said. "I want to pay for the eggs." He gestured. "Tell me how much. Jones always pays, so I don't know."

"That's three hundred dollars."

He looked at the bills in his hand. "Is it okay? I have more."

"Where on earth did you get it? Did you rob a bank?"

"No, the Department of State," he said. "US Department of State. They pay fifty thousand dollars to every Soviet pilot who gives them a MiG."

"Fifty thousand dollars."

"Yeah. I guess they said a crashed MiG is okay."

"You're carrying *fifty thousand dollars* in your coat pockets."

"Ten thousand only. Ten big ones." He gave me a quick glance, as if looking to see whether I had caught the slang. "Not enough pockets for fifty thousand."

"Where is the rest?"

"I left it," he said. "In my room at the base. I had to leave it." He made a brave attempt at that grin. "If Jones is smart, he'll tell them I took all of it."

I had never seen three hundred dollars all at once in my life, not even in the travelers' checks Dad took out when we first moved to Germany—certainly not in bills. I couldn't begin to get my mind around the thought that he had ten thousand dollars in that suit coat. Surely the State Department wouldn't just give him fifty thousand dollars cash stuffed in a suitcase like casino winnings. Surely somebody—Agent Jones?—would have explained to him about bank accounts and checkbooks if he didn't know. Why on earth was it all in cash?

Unless—

Unless he knew he was going to be on the run.

I set the eggs carefully on the counter. My heart was in my throat; my stomach was tying itself in knots. "Do you have any idea how much money ten thousand dollars is?"

Another slow shake of the head. Another uncertain glance at the bills in his hand. "I don't know American money yet. Jones always pays."

"It's more than Dad makes in a year, and he's O-6. That's the highest pay grade for a field officer."

He looked taken aback. "A lot of money."

"A lot of money."

He looked at me quickly. He must have heard the tightness in my voice.

"It's for my house," he said, then corrected himself a little. "It was supposed to be for my house. The Air Force—they wanted me to stay here and . . . consult? To help with the research on the base. And Jones says because I will be a 'civilian consultant,' I don't have to live on the base if I don't want. I can live in my own house. We pay in cash so they don't trace it."

"So who doesn't trace it?"

"KGB," he said. "Jones says we pay in cash so KGB don't trace it. In case they try to find me."

It was the second time he had said something about "KGB" just now. "What is KGB?" I asked. "Like the CIA? Your version of the CIA?"

"They're not mine. They are Russian. I am not Russian." His voice was hard. "KGB are killers. In the war, we called them NKVD, but they're the same. Killers. Bastards. *Vyrodky*."

I remembered Jo's story about the Red assassin with the cigarette-case gun. It made sense, I thought, that the Reds would want to stop Maksym from spilling secrets about weapons or air tactics or whatever else a defecting pilot might spill secrets about; it made sense that they would try to find him and silence him. It made sense that he had anticipated needing to live practically in hiding, paying for everything in cash.

The knots in my stomach loosened a little.

"Well, you don't need to pay me three hundred dollars for breakfast," I told him.

"Not only for breakfast," he said. "Also for the trouble."

"We're not in trouble yet," I said.

NINE

I MISSED THE NINE O'CLOCK bus to downtown by about ten seconds. It was just disappearing around the bend when I reached the corner of Floyd Avenue. The buses only ran every two hours in summer. For a moment, I thought about going over to Jo's to see whether she was home and could drive me, but I didn't want to be stuck explaining why I suddenly needed elastic bandages and cotton balls and antiseptic when I didn't have a scratch on me. I didn't think she was the type to let it go without question.

I started walking.

I wouldn't have minded normally. This was a good stretch for walking. The river was nearby, close enough that you could hear the warble of the water, and there were wild daisies and black-eyed Susans nodding along the roadside, and the air was full of birdsong and the smell of honeysuckle and summer-sweet. But it was breathtakingly hot and humid—the sidewalk had been baking in direct sun all morning—and I had made the mistake of trying to dress up a little, burying my jittery nerves under careful layers of makeup and tulle. The nylon crinoline under my skirt was sticking to my legs within five minutes. My blouse was soaked down the back and plastered to my skin.

I stopped at the Esso station on the corner of Floyd and Oakwood to make my first two purchases—a Rome *Sentinel* and a New York State road map. The paper was for room listings. I couldn't see any way around it: Maksym couldn't stay at the house, which meant taking out a room. We could use his money to pay for it—we would have to use his money; I surely didn't have the money to rent a room—but I would have to be the one making the arrangements, and the room would be under my name. An alias, of course, but *my* alias.

It was nerve-racking to think about. But I had made my choice.

The map was his request. He wanted to work out a route to Toronto—to Toronto specifically. He had taken a neatly folded handbill from his breast pocket and given it to me to look at over the breakfast table.

*Ukrainian Canadian Relief Fund—Bloor Street West, Toronto, Ontario, Canada—assistance to refugees and displaced persons—resettlement assistance—*printed first in English and then in what I assumed was Ukrainian.

The paper was yellow and brittle, starting to wear through at the creases. "Where did you get this?" I asked.

"They gave it to me. After the war—in the camp, UN camp. They gave it to me."

"You've been carrying this since the war?"

"I think maybe they will help me," he said.

I shook my head and gave it back to him. "Canadian police are looking for you too. They'll just send you back."

He had acknowledged this with one short nod, his face blank as he folded the paper up very carefully and returned it to his breast pocket. But I could tell that had shattered him a little.

I decided to bring him his map anyway.

The customer ahead of me, a young guy in a sharp, expensive-looking suit and with enough pomade in his slick black hair to cause temporary blindness, lounged at the counter, leaning easily on his elbows. He had to be even hotter in that wool suit than I was in my crinoline, but he was chattering away happily in Italian with the wizened little clerk as he paid for his Coca-Cola bottles. Neither seemed to be in any particular hurry, so I was left studying the bulletin board on the wall behind the counter while I waited, fanning myself with the map, slowly asphyxiating on the smell of hot tire rubber and gasoline—nearly jumping when I found Maksym grinning back at me from the flyer in the middle of the board.

WANTED BY THE FBI, read the text in big block letters over his head; and then, in slightly smaller type just beneath, ESPIONAGE—UNLAWFUL FLIGHT; and then his name underneath the photograph: MAKSYM IVANOVYCH KOSTYSHYN. They had finally gotten it right.

A description ran below. I had to edge forward a little and squint to read it.

Born September 2, 1933, Kulikov, USSR; Height, 5'10"—they were being generous with that one—*Weight, 140 pounds; Hair, dark brown; Eyes, brown; Race, white; Nationality, Soviet; Scars and marks, scar left forearm, surgical scar left side abdomen, multiple scars back . . .*

The list of scars went on and on—why were there so many?—but it was that birth date that made my stomach turn over uneasily. *September 2, 1933.* I wasn't sure how old I thought he was—mid to late twenties, if I had to guess. I supposed I had assumed he just looked very young for his age. But he was only three years older than I was. He had only been eleven when the European war ended in May 1945.

It's not training, he said. *It's what we did during the war.*

He was too young to have fought in the war.

I must have misunderstood him. He must have meant it generally, *we* as in *my people*, as in *It's what we Ukrainians did during the war.*

Or he had been lying.

He grinned down at me from the flyer, blithe and dimpled and clean-cut with his cheekbones and jawline to die for. That grin. Such a stupid photograph for a wanted flyer. It looked like a publicity shot. I guessed it probably was. They had probably planned to use it on propaganda leaflets dropped in daring flyovers at the edges of Red airspace all over the world. *Look*, the leaflets would say in Russian and Polish and Chinese and Korean, *look how happy this pilot is. Look how well he's being treated. He defected to the United States of America to enjoy a better life, and so can you!*

"Miss?" the little clerk said. The counter was vacated. "Miss?"

I paid for my newspaper and road map and headed back out into the stifling heat. Hair Pomade Guy was getting into the passenger's side of a handsome falcon-gray Pontiac sedan at one of the gasoline pumps. The driver's door swung open as I passed.

"Miss Blaine," Agent Jones said.

I very nearly kept walking. At the last second, I thought better of it. I turned slowly around, fighting the urge to hide the paper and the map behind my back.

"Yes," I said—a statement, clipped and cold, not a question, to make it clear I wasn't inviting anything else from him. My insides were clenched like a fist. Oh God, that stupid telephone call, the way I had hung up on him—what I had said when I hung up on him. Had it only been last night? It felt like ages. That was a different girl, not me. That was the girl who didn't have a federal fugitive on her living room sofa.

He stood there with a hand on the Pontiac's doorframe, silently taking me in, so I returned the favor. He was tall and tanned and fit, like an athlete, like somebody who spent more time out-of-doors than in, somebody you would expect to see posing proudly with a rainbow trout on the cover of *Western Sportsman*, or on brochures for safari tours in the Kalahari or mountain-climbing expeditions in the Himalayas—somebody who apparently had a conscientious objection to dress codes. His suit coat was off again today, shirt sleeves rolled to the elbow, though he wore hat and tie. The brim of his fedora was pulled low, shading his face. His eyes were bluish-greenish gray, nearly the same color as the car, flat and hard and cool as slate tiles. You couldn't tell what he was thinking.

"Want a lift?" he asked suddenly.

It caught me off guard. "Excuse me?"

"Are you going to walk, or do you want a lift?"

I hesitated. It was too late for pride. I was sure he had already filed away every last detail of my appearance—soaked blouse, melting crinoline, flushed face. Had he noted the map too? Would he ask about it, *given the circumstances*? But it would be suspicious not to accept the ride. It was blazing hot—and anyway, I had every right to walk to a filling station and purchase a road map. I had just moved to the area, after all. And I had the feeling he would be much less likely than Jo to pry into what I needed from the drugstore. In my experience, men tended not to want to know things like that.

I lifted my chin. "You're going downtown?"

"Base. But I can drop you downtown. Unless you want to go to base."

Hair Pomade Guy's shiny head popped out suddenly from the passenger window.

"Hey, you can ride shotgun," he called. "I'll sit in the back."

"Just to the drugstore, thank you," I told Agent Jones tightly.

He walked around to hold the passenger door for me without a word. Hair Pomade Guy, relocated to the back, stuck a hand out to me over the seat as I climbed stiffly in.

"Mancuso," he said.

I thought he was probably a few years older than Maksym—twenty-four or twenty-five. I put my newspaper and map on the floor, where they would be out of Agent Jones's sight. I made sure there wasn't any ink smudged on my palms and took Agent Mancuso's hand. He shook mine rather enthusiastically, giving me a broad, friendly smile. He had a very firm grip.

"What does it mean?" I asked him. "Shotgun?"

Agent Jones, dropping into the driver's seat and turning over the engine, said shortly, "Means he reads too many pulp Westerns." His hand on the gear lever was bruised rather conspicuously across the knuckles. It was reassuring in a sick sort of way. Maksym had been telling the truth about one thing, at least.

"Okay," Agent Mancuso said, "so, you know—a stagecoach? You've got the one guy holding the reins, and you've got that other guy sitting up there with a shotgun, looking out for the bad guys. That's riding shotgun." He winked at me, and I smiled at him reflexively. "Important job. Better keep an eye out."

We pulled out onto Floyd Avenue. "Goddamn, it's hot," Agent Mancuso said, then coughed and said, "Sorry, ma'am. Gosh darn, it's hot. I thought they said it was supposed to be cooler upstate. Hotter here than the city." I heard the *plink* of a bottle cap. One of his Coca-Cola bottles drifted toward me over the seat. "Want one?"

"That's okay," I said.

"Come on—before they get flat." He floated the bottle back and forth enticingly. "It's got to be you. Jones ain't touching nothing below one hundred proof."

"You bought two bottles," I pointed out. "You're sure one of them wasn't for him?"

"Nah—two bottles for seven cents. Couldn't pass up a good deal. That's Italians for you."

"That's marketing," Agent Jones said.

"Come on," Agent Mancuso said. "They ain't lasting till Toronto."

The fist in my stomach tightened a little. "Toronto?"

"Here, drink up."

I took the bottle, numbly compliant. The glass was still frosted all over from the icebox except where Agent Mancuso's fingers had left marks. "What's in Toronto?" I asked. The coincidence made me uneasy. Did they know about that leaflet in Maksym's breast pocket—the *Ukrainian Canadian Relief Fund*? Had they guessed Maksym would try going there for help?

"Pretty good ball team," Agent Mancuso said easily, "the Maple Leafs—same as the hockey team. Do they have some kind of rule or something? Every team in Toronto's got to be the Maple Leafs." He said it like *Tor-ah-no*. "Maybe not a rule. They just don't have nothing else up there to name a team after. Except moose." He caught my eye in the side mirror and winked again.

"I've got some leads in Toronto," Agent Jones said.

I clenched the bottle tightly between my hands. It started to sweat condensation rapidly, the ice flaking off and melting into little rivulets between my fingers. I wiped my hands on my skirt. "On the Russian."

"That's right."

I tipped the bottle up and took a deliberate, measured sip, willing my hand not to shake. "How far is Toronto?"

"Three hundred miles," Agent Jones said, "give or take ten. Flight'll take an hour. Five hours if we were driving."

"Five if it's him driving," Agent Mancuso put in, leaning on his elbows over the seat. "Four if it's me."

"How far is that in kilometers?"

Agent Jones gave me an odd little sidelong look.

"I've lived in Germany since I was eleven," I said. "I'm more used to the metric system."

"That doesn't change the travel time," he said.

We had managed to be civil so far, but now I felt the sudden need to dash my Coca-Cola into his expressionless, tanned face. I took another sip instead, to give my hands something else to do. "I'm just wondering how he's supposed to have made three hundred miles on a broken ankle in less than twenty-four hours."

He braked for the stoplight at Garden Street. "How do you know he's got a broken ankle?"

A bloom of panic filled my throat. I swallowed it carefully back down. "Agent Kimball—the FBI officer. He says they think he probably broke an ankle when he jumped out of that window on base."

"Uh-huh," Agent Jones said. "Do you mind?" With his bruised hand, he took a pack of cigarettes and a Zippo lighter from his breast pocket.

I shook my head mutely.

"Want one?"

"No, thank you," I said through clenched teeth.

"Dean?"

"Hey—if you're offering," Agent Mancuso said. "Thanks."

Agent Jones shook out a cigarette for Agent Mancuso and another for himself.

"I didn't say he walked himself to Toronto," he said to me, flicking the cap of the lighter smoothly and dipping his head to light the cigarette. He shut the lighter and returned it to his pocket.

"Yep, he's got help, no question," Agent Mancuso said.

The light turned green.

"What kind of help?" I asked, holding on to my Coca-Cola bottle tightly.

"Well—let's just say we, uh, found some compromising material when we turned his room over," Agent Mancuso said.

"Addresses on a slip of paper in one of his bags," Agent Jones said to me levelly.

"Addresses?"

"Addresses, instructions for intelligence drops," Agent Mancuso supplied, seizing on an opportunity. He seemed bursting to talk about it. "You know—passwords, signals. That kind of stuff. 'Contact will be smoking a pipe and holding a newspaper.' Textbook stuff."

"These were addresses in Toronto?" I guessed.

"Couple of 'em Toronto, couple of 'em Syracuse. Couple

other places." Agent Mancuso took an excited drag on his cigarette. "Know what else we found? Fifty thousand dollars cash."

"Wow," I managed.

It sounded weak even to me. Agent Jones gave me another little sidelong look, his blue-green eyes empty.

"Fifty thousand dollars *cash*," Agent Mancuso repeated, shaking his head as if he couldn't quite believe it himself. "A lot of dough."

I swallowed another sip of Coca-Cola without tasting it. There should have been only forty thousand; the rest was currently in the lining of Maksym's suit coat. But of course I shouldn't have known that. They shouldn't have been telling me any of this stuff either. Maybe Agent Mancuso was a rookie and didn't know any better; maybe he was just running his mouth because he enjoyed having an audience to impress. But I didn't doubt for one second that Agent Jones knew exactly what he was doing. He had caught my stupid slipup about Maksym's ankle.

He was setting out traps; that was what he was doing. He was seeing whether he could trip me up again.

"So you think somebody in Syracuse or Toronto is hiding him," I said.

"Doesn't have to be somebody in Syracuse or Toronto," Agent Mancuso said. "Probably isn't, matter of fact. They were probably just planning to make the drops there. The point is, he ain't acting alone. He's got somebody on the outside."

"Another Red agent, you mean."

"Well—what we would call the case officer. The guy running the show." Agent Mancuso leaned on his elbows on the seat, pulling happily on his cigarette. "It's a neat little setup. Our Russki pilot gathers the material on base, passes it along to the case officer, whoever he is—"

"Or she," Agent Jones said, looking at me.

"That's true," Agent Mancuso allowed. "Could be a woman. Anyway, right on up the line it goes—right to Moscow." He waved an illustrative hand. "That's what makes these espionage networks so damn hard to break up—sorry, ma'am. So hard to break up. Normally, these people—these low-level guys, the ones doing the legwork—normally, they don't know each other. They don't know the other operatives—the other agents. Maybe they don't even know their case officer. They don't know names or looks or nothing. So even if you nab one of them, they can't give you nothing about the rest of the network. Normally, a guy like our pilot doesn't know nothing about who he's passing the stuff to—nothing but a cover name and an address or two, maybe some passwords so he can make the drops. Normally." He gave me a brilliant grin. "But we caught a break with this guy."

I looked at the Coca-Cola bottle in my hands and said, "Why is that?"

"Because they pulled him out," Agent Jones said around his cigarette.

"What?"

"I said because they pulled him out." He took out his cigarette and held it in two fingers over the steering wheel. "They pulled him out when they realized Air Force intelligence was flagging up those photos of his MiG, knocking holes in his cover story. Means he must have made contact with his case officer at some point while he was on base. Possibly through a third party. In any case, probably through somebody at that dance Wednesday night." He flicked the ash from the tip of his cigarette out the window.

"I've been meaning to ask you, Miss Blaine," he said. "What did he talk to you about?"

My stomach turned over. I clenched the Coca-Cola bottle tightly. "Nothing," I said. "I forgot my pipe and newspaper."

Agent Mancuso laughed. Agent Jones didn't. He put his cigarette back in his mouth, cheeks hollowing as he took a drag. His face was stone blank.

"Do you think I'm his contact, Agent Jones?" I asked him. I said it lightly—just making a joke. But neither of us was joking just then. My heart was thudding so loudly that I was sure he could hear it, even over the rush of wind through the open windows.

"No," Agent Jones said. "But I think he thought you were."

TEN

THE THING WAS, IT MADE a certain amount of sense.

It would explain why he had approached me in the first place—me, out of everybody at that party. It would explain the spilled champagne. It was a whole lot easier to believe he had been deliberately creating an excuse to linger at my table than to believe it had just been a clumsy accident. He was a test pilot; surely he couldn't afford to be clumsy.

It might even explain why he had come to the house in Birchwood.

But it didn't explain last night. It didn't explain his begging me to believe him; it didn't explain his fear. He hadn't thought I was his contact or his case officer. He had thought I was going to turn him in.

"I don't know if I can remember it all in order," I said to Agent Jones.

"Give it a shot," he said.

"He thought I was asking him for a drink. He brought me a drink. I didn't know who he was until he said something about Dad doing his debriefing. And then he said you didn't like him talking to reporters. At least . . ." I hesitated, try-ing to put the jumbled fragments of the conversation back together. "He said you were answering the press questions because his English wasn't good, and I said actually it was pretty good—"

"That Russki's got better English than I do," Agent Mancuso put in.

"—and then he said you always told reporters his English wasn't very good because you didn't like him talking to reporters."

"Part of his asylum deal," Agent Jones said around his cigarette.

"What?"

He took out the cigarette with slightly exaggerated patience and said, "Part of the deal we made for him with Copenhagen. They've got their own agreement with Moscow that says NATO keeps hands off Bornholm. They don't want to publicize that they gave us the pilot. So—part of the asylum deal. If we want Kostyshyn, we keep his mouth shut. No press."

His voice was cool and dry. He sounded somewhere between annoyed and diabolically amused. Maksym was probably going to be front page on every newspaper on the East Coast by tonight. So much for no press.

He flicked a sidelong glance at me. "Was that it?"

"He told me his name. He explained a little about his name. He said they got it wrong on his citizenship papers, his American citizenship papers. They just said 'Maksym Ivanovych' because they thought Ivanovych was the surname. But he said you told him it was probably better that they didn't use his real surname anyway." I shrugged lightly. "He asked if I danced."

Agent Mancuso leaned on his elbows, exhaling smoke contentedly. "What'd you tell him?"

"I said I was wearing the wrong dress."

"I bet that was the line," Agent Mancuso said. "I bet that was him trying to confirm you were his girl. You'd have something specific you were supposed to say back to him at that point, see."

"Or he wanted a dance," Agent Jones said. "Anything else?"

It reminded me a little of what Jo had said yesterday— *Probably just wanted a normal conversation for a change.* I shook my head and looked out the window. I was suddenly afraid of what he might see in my face. "That was it. You came and got him. He said good night."

We had pulled up along the curb in front of Goldberg's department store. The drugstore was across the street. Agent Jones put on the hand brake, took one last unhurried drag, and flicked his cigarette butt out the window.

"Need a cab fare?" he asked.

"I'm sorry?"

"For the ride back. Need the fare?"

It wasn't so much the things he said; it was the way he said them, all in that same bland, dry monotone and with that flat, blank look in his eyes, as if nothing in this world had ever surprised him or would ever surprise him—and yet at the same time you couldn't help feeling he was laughing at you behind that poker face. It had me constantly wrong-footed. I supposed that was intentional.

"It's fine. I'll wait for the bus," I said.

He was already opening his wallet, turning his back to me.

"I said it's fine," I said a little more sharply. "I don't need money."

He ignored me. He took a ballpoint pen and a memo pad from his breast pocket and made a show of making himself a note; I supposed he was required to itemize his expenses. Then he folded a couple of bills with infuriating deliberation, put them in my hand, and got out, slamming his door shut.

"Yeah," Agent Mancuso said sagely from the back seat, wreathed in smoke like an oracle, "you weren't gonna win that fight. He's John Wayne outside and Roy Rogers inside. Don't tell him I said that."

I sat there for a moment with the money in my hand, stunned and flushed and simmering, hating Agent Jones and his stony, tanned face and his cool slate eyes that knew too much and revealed nothing—and then, as my fingers clenched into a fist, they closed around some small, flat, solid object folded neatly and carefully between the bills.

I froze.

Agent Jones opened my door from the sidewalk and stood waiting for me to get out.

I bent very slowly to pick up my newspaper and map. I slid off the hot leather seat, mouth dry.

"Good day, Miss Blaine," Agent Jones said, giving me that curt little nod of his.

They drove off, Agent Mancuso having reclaimed shotgun duties. I stood there on the curb and unfolded the bills with shaking fingers. A slip of white paper fluttered down to the sidewalk. A thin, cool metal fob dropped into my palm with a silvery jangle.

PAUL REVERE MOTOR HOTEL

HWY. 26

ROME, N.Y.

RM. 72

And there was a room key.

I swooped to snatch up the piece of paper, heart in my throat. It was the timetable for the daily early express train from New York City.

New York Central System
Adv. Empire State Exp.
Lve. New York Gd. Cent. Term. (E. T.) AM 4:40
Arr. Albany 7:00
Lve. Albany 7:05
Arr. Rome 9:07
Lve. Rome 9:12

It ended there. It had evidently been torn out from a larger table. It looked like any ordinary, meaningless bit of accumulated scrap paper, shoved into his wallet and mixed up with the bills by accident—except he had penned the word *ethanol* in the space along the edge. One word in a sharp, sure hand, all small capitals. There wasn't anything else. The reverse was blank.

Nothing Agent Jones did was an accident. That key wasn't an accident.

Slowly, I dug in my purse for my pocketbook and slipped his two dollars in with the five I had scrounged from our grocery money—hopefully enough for an elastic bandage for Maksym's ankle and antiseptic for those worrisome ugly cuts on his hands. I couldn't use Maksym's money, though he had offered. He didn't have anything smaller than hundreds.

I ran my thumb over the etching on the key fob. PAUL REVERE MOTOR HOTEL, RM. 72. It wasn't Agent Jones's room—at least, it wasn't the room he was staying over in. He had been with Maksym in the officers' dorm on base.

There wasn't a single savory reason I could think of for why a man would discreetly slip me a motel key. I could probably take this to the police station and have him cited for indecency. But what sort of man invited a girl for a tryst by slipping her a note about *ethanol*?

Fingers still shaking a little, I zipped up the room key and the baffling scrap of paper in my pocketbook and went across the street to the drugstore.

Maksym's flyer was taped up on the door, between the OPEN card and a poster advertising Old Gold cigarettes—*If you want a Treat instead of a Treatment . . . Old Gold treats you right!* I was the only customer, and the druggist disappeared into the back to take a telephone call after he had finished wrapping up my purchases: $1.92 for a rolled Ace bandage, a package of cotton balls, a box of Band-Aids, and one fluid ounce of tincture of merthiolate. I took the flyer down and stuffed it quickly into my handbag. Somehow, that felt more criminal than the fact that MAKSYM IVANOVYCH KOSTYSHYN, WANTED BY THE FBI, was holed up in my house, waiting for me to bring him medical supplies and a road map.

I escaped back out onto the sidewalk and waved over a cab from the Goldberg's pool.

"Where to?" asked the cabbie, looking up at me in the mirror as I settled myself into the back seat.

I looked at my wristwatch. Nine thirty. I hadn't expected to get back to the house before ten once I'd resigned myself to walking; I thought it would take me an hour at least.

I had $5.08 in my pocketbook. The rate on the meter said 25¢ FIRST 1/5 MILE, 5¢ EVERY 1/5 MILE AFTER.

I swallowed my heart back down into my chest and said, "How far to the Paul Revere?"

ELEVEN

I WAS BRACING MYSELF FOR the worst—the seediest, shabbiest, most isolated hourly-rate motel you could think of. But the Paul Revere Motor Hotel was right on the state route and clearly targeted toward tourists: a sprawling building in Colonial Revival style, red brick and white columns and cupolas like a reproduction Monticello, flung out expansively across an immaculate emerald lawn. A horseshoe driveway looped past the office and back out to the highway. The white-washed wooden sign before the entrance said THE PAUL REVERE MOTOR HOTEL in stately serif capitals—and then underneath, not quite as stately, TV—PRIVATE POOL—TENNIS & GOLF.

I paid the cabbie, scooped my things off the seat, and went in through the tall double doors, half nerves and half gnawing curiosity.

A blast of frosty air-conditioning hit me just inside the doors, and I stood there for a moment luxuriating in it. The lobby was all flagstone and wood panels and exposed beams, cozily rustic. At left was the check-in counter; at right lay a sunken lounge with a scattering of wing chairs and ottomans and an enormous stone fireplace, complete with an old-fashioned crane arm for holding a kettle over the fire. An archway at the far end of the lounge led, I assumed, into the restaurant and bar; a pair of French doors at the back of the lobby opened to the pool courtyard.

The check-in girl was occupied with a flock of middle-aged ladies in sporty Lacoste golf dresses and visors and slim leather gloves and kilted shoes. A lone couple were deep in conversation over their coffee cups in the lounge. I passed unnoticed through the lobby and slipped out through the French doors to the courtyard.

The pool didn't open until ten o'clock. The courtyard was empty and rather forlorn, the umbrellas closed up, the deck chairs neatly folded and stacked. The motel rooms flanked the courtyard in two long wings on either side of the office. A painted sign pointed out the room numbers in each direction: 1–35 to the left, 36–70 to the right.

Only 1 through 70. My key was for Room 72.

I followed the walkway slowly down to the end of each wing and back, looking at each brass number on each door just in case, as if I expected the nonexistent Room 72 to magically appear; and then, unwilling to accept defeat, I walked around the pool and let myself through the chain-link gate in the tall juniper hedge on the far side. Perhaps there were more rooms back here.

Beyond the junipers, a gravel path ran between the vacant tennis courts and the parking lot to a cluster of freestanding clapboard buildings just beneath the eaves of the encroaching pinewood. Another painted sign said CABINS, 71–75.

Not a room, then. An entire cabin.

Number 72 was farthest from the path and closest to the woods, half hidden behind Number 71. I climbed up onto the narrow, railed porch, heart thumping. You couldn't see the main building from here, just the line of junipers marching off past the tennis courts. You couldn't hear the highway. At this moment, it could have been me alone in the world—me and whatever was behind this door, whatever Agent Jones wanted me and no one else to know about.

I knocked and waited, listening. Then, slowly and deliberately, hands sweating, I unzipped my pocketbook, took out the key, and unlocked the door.

Sunlight rushed in around me as I pushed the door open, scattering dust motes, chasing shadows away across the floor and up the wood-paneled walls. I stepped slowly inside, leaving the door open behind me—I knew better than to let myself be shut in—and switched on the overhead light.

The place looked perfectly ordinary. It reminded me a bit of the cabins we used to stay in at Hinterzarten in the Black Forest each Christmas; I supposed cabins looked much the same wherever they were. There was a kitchenette—sink, compact refrigerator, card table with two folding chairs—and a little sitting area with a matched mahogany settee and rocker on a braided scrap rug. Most of the right-hand wall was taken up with an enormous woodstove. A door on the far wall led to the bedroom—queen bed, dresser, desk and chair, all in mahogany—and the tiny bath. The faint tang of Pine-Sol and musty damp hung on the still air. Everything was neatly made up, unused and untouched, clean and bare and empty—no water stains on the bathroom counter, no wet towels on the rack, nothing in the wastepaper baskets.

It was too early for housekeeping to have come by. Nobody had been here, plain and simple.

I dropped my things on the settee and spent a few minutes going through the kitchen and bedroom, opening up drawers and looking in cabinets, finding nothing but the Gideon Bible in the top dresser drawer. Defeated, I sank onto the edge of the bed. Had somebody else gotten here first and found whatever I was supposed to find? Or was this all some elaborate test I had somehow failed?

Maybe it had just been a trick—slipping me the key. Maybe Agent Jones was just seeing whether I would say something about it. Maybe I had confirmed some hunch of his when I hadn't.

My stomach jumped.

He had caught my slipup about Maksym's ankle. He was just getting me out of the way so they could go to Birchwood and search the house.

No wonder he had been laughing at me behind that poker face. I had fallen for it so easily.

I couldn't even work up the energy to be angry. I fought an inexplicable urge to laugh.

I found my feet somehow. Numbly, I gathered my things from the settee, switched off the light, and went back outside, shutting the door to Number 72 behind me.

"A cab, please," I said to the check-in girl back in the office. My heart was stuck in a tight knot at the base of my throat. I half expected to hear police sirens out on the highway. They must have found Maksym by now. Agent Jones would know where to find me.

The check-in girl was about my age, tall and trim in her cheery sunflower-yellow rayon suit and pillbox hat. She gave me an apologetic smile as she reached for her telephone. "I'll have to call somebody up from the downtown stand," she told me. "We've only got the one cab on call here, and that golfing party wanted to drive over to the first tee—all nine of them! It's only half a mile—but of course it's so hot."

"It is hot," I murmured vaguely.

"It'll be ten minutes or so. I'm sorry. I can have the car sent around if you'd rather wait in your room."

"No, that's fine," I said—and then, as the thought occurred: "Actually—could you check to see if there are any messages for me? Number seventy-two." I laid my key on the counter.

She held the receiver on her shoulder while she ran her fingers over the row of mailboxes. "Oh, yes—Mrs. Kobryn! We weren't sure exactly when to expect you. Your husband seemed to think you'd be getting in this afternoon."

Mrs. Kobryn?

I dropped my left hand off the counter so she wouldn't see the bare ring finger.

"Yes," I said hoarsely. "Yes, I got in a little early."

"Is the room satisfactory?"

"Very satisfactory, thank you." I swallowed against the knot in my throat. "I'm so sorry—could you remind me how long the reservation is for? How many nights?"

"Just the two—last night and tonight. We did have to charge for last night even though nobody was in the room." She looked a little embarrassed. "Mr. Kobryn wanted to go ahead and make the reservation even though you weren't getting in until today. He wanted that cabin in particular—seventy-two—and we couldn't hold it without the reservation. It's policy, unfortunately."

"That's all right."

"No messages—I'm sorry." Another apologetic smile. "I'll call that cab for you."

I slumped into one of the wing chairs in the lounge to wait. *Mrs. Kobryn.* Was I supposed to be Mrs. Kobryn? Or if not me, then who? (Was Agent Jones Mr. Kobryn?) Why Cabin 72 in particular? And what sort of name was *Kobryn* anyway? It was like trying to put together a thousand-piece jigsaw puzzle, except a quarter of the pieces were missing, another quarter were from an entirely different puzzle, and you weren't allowed to look at the picture on either box. I had no idea whether Agent Jones was trying to trap me or trying to help me; I had no idea whether Maksym was a genuine defector or a Red spy; and I had no idea what any of this had to do with ethanol.

"Hey, good-looking! What's cooking?"

Jo Matheson alighted on the arm of a nearby wing chair, picture perfect in a dazzling white golf dress and flawless makeup, Ray-Bans perched just so atop her glossy brunette tousle.

I straightened reflexively, as if I had just been told to mind my manners and sit up at the dinner table. I was wearing my best skirt and blouse and pumps, but I still felt ungainly and childish next to her, and for the first time I felt a little sour about it. Just in case I wasn't feeling low enough, here was Jo Matheson with her perfect makeup and her engineering degree and her long, tanned legs. Agent Jones should try his little key trick on her. I bet she could figure him out.

"Hi, yourself," I said.

"Don't sound so excited." Her gaze roved over the collection of stuff in my lap, settling on the brown paper package from the drugstore. "Are you running dope?"

I hadn't given any thought to a cover story. I knew exactly one person in Rome, not counting the Soviet spy in my living room, and of course it was just my luck that she would be here in the same exact twenty-minute window of time as I.

"Just errands," I said tightly. "I found a key on the sidewalk downtown. I came by to drop it off."

She arched a sculpted brow. "Please tell me you didn't come all the way up here to drop off a key."

"It's my good deed for the day."

"You know you could have just slipped it in a mailbox? That's why they put the address on the fob. They cover the postage."

"Oh," I said.

"Well, now you're here," she said. "How about brunch?"

"What?"

"I'm starving. I just finished walking a full round. I should have been done an hour ago, but there were two poky four-somes ahead of me who wouldn't let me play through. Took me ages to finish, and I'm starving." She shot up from the arm of the chair. "Come on. They've got Friday brunch at the restaurant here."

"I'm supposed to be waiting for a cab," I said.

"Forget the cab."

"I should probably—"

"Oh, stop being such a stick-in-the-mud. Your dad said I could keep you out until eleven as long as we don't touch a drop of gin."

I made an utterly unconvincing attempt at a smile.

"Come on. I'm treating," Jo said.

"ALL RIGHT," JO SAID, "WHAT'S up, Blaine, really?"

We sat on the terrace of the motel restaurant—called The Beeches rather inexplicably. All the trees on the grounds seemed to be pines. Geriatric lawn bowlers milled in murmuring little clusters on the green below us. Friday was apparently match day.

I swallowed a mouthful of watery iced coffee and willed my foot to stop tapping. The type of people who did weekday brunches evidently weren't the type of people to be in a hurry about anything; at least Jo wasn't. She had ordered the full country breakfast—eggs, toast, bacon, potatoes. I had ordered the continental—one buttered roll, choice of hot or iced coffee—and had finished twenty minutes ago. I was sitting there sweating and stewing in nerves and impatience while Jo spread marmalade leisurely over another piece of toast.

"Nothing. I just didn't know about the postage thing," I said.

She divided her toast into pieces with neatly manicured fingers, the nails glossy red as if they had been dipped in liquid vermilion. I had no idea how she could play a round of golf with her nails looking like that. I could break a nail buttoning my blouse.

"That's not what I'm talking about. You've said a total of five words since we sat down. You've been checking your watch every thirty seconds." She slipped one tiny sliver of marmalade-laden toast into her mouth—slowly and delicately, as if she were sampling hors d'oeuvres at the Ritz-Carlton. "Spill it. I know when something's bugging you."

"You've known me for less than a week," I said crabbily.

"Well, that's how obvious you're being."

"It's just hot," I said.

"Spill it," she ordered.

She was like a bloodhound. I couldn't tell her about the cabin or the note or about "Mrs. Kobryn," not without having to explain everything, but I had to give her something to shake her off the scent. I bent reluctantly to take Maksym's flyer out of my handbag. I pushed it slowly to her across the table, as though I were letting her in on some deep and shameful secret.

She smoothed the flyer out over the tabletop.

"Well, I guess they haven't found him," she said. "And that poor FBI guy was so sure they would. What was his name?"

"Maksym."

"I know the commie is Maksym, darling. His name's on this thing. I meant that FBI guy."

"Oh," I said. "Kimball."

"Kimball. Poor old Kimball." She was silent for a moment, looking over the flyer. "He does have a nice smile, doesn't he? The commie, not Kimball."

"I almost danced with him," I confessed in a low voice. "Wednesday night. He wanted me to dance with him."

She snorted. "Is that why you've got the mopes? Please. How were you supposed to know? Of course he did. Of course he's going to be the perfect gentleman. That's why they send guys like him. You're not supposed to suspect him. You're supposed to think, 'That guy, a commie spy? Never. He's so nice! He's got such a nice smile!' That's the whole point.

"You know," she said, leaning in on her elbows and selecting another piece of toast, "he was probably supposed to get close to an American girl. It was probably part of his mission— get her to fall for him so he could use her as a front. Get her to scrounge supplies for him." She tipped crumbs right onto Maksym's handsome face, as if to emphasize her point. "Well, guess what? Too bad for him he tried it on Shelby Blaine."

I folded the flyer up, brushing off the crumbs, and returned it to my handbag. My fingers were numb.

"Too bad for him," I said.

TWELVE

I ENDED UP HAVING TO take a cab back to the house after all, as Jo had something or other to do on the other side of town before her bridge club at two o'clock and didn't have the time to drive to Birchwood and back and then back again. I kept thinking over what she had said the whole way home, and the fist in my stomach kept tightening.

He was probably supposed to get close to an American girl. It was probably part of his mission. Get her to scrounge supplies for him. Get her to fall for him.

I had that flyer with his birth date—concrete proof that he had deliberately lied to me at least once. And now I knew he had been keeping things from me too, lying by omission. They had found those addresses in his bags, Syracuse and Toronto addresses. To be fair, he had shown me a Toronto address. But he hadn't said a word about Syracuse, even when I told him that was where they were looking for him.

Whatever or whoever was in Syracuse, he didn't want me knowing.

He was asleep on the sofa, stretched out on his stomach with his face dug into the crook of his left arm, his right arm folded under his chest. He twitched a little when I flipped the light on and dumped my things onto the coffee table, but he didn't lift his head. He lay still, his breathing low and shivery. His coat was off. The back of his shirt was drenched with sweat.

"Maksym," I said.

No movement. No sound except his labored breathing. I was too irritated to wait. I bent over him, right over the back of his close-shaven head, and snapped, "Maksym."

He turned his head onto his cheek, opening his eyes. In the same movement, stiff and careful, he unfolded his right arm from under his chest. He had the pistol in his hand.

He lodged the muzzle against my stomach, just below my breastbone.

I froze.

"Maksym—"

"*Moskalka*," he breathed, voice choked. He swallowed and muttered something else, low and bitter and incomprehensible; then he looked up into my face and repeated, "*Moskalka*."

I didn't dare move. I stood there against the muzzle of that pistol. This wasn't like yesterday in the kitchen. This wasn't fear. His hand was trembling, almost spasmodic. His eyes were dark with fever, the pupils dilated wide. His face was pale and sweat-sheened.

He was in pain, and he was furious.

"Maksym," I whispered, "it's me—it's Shelby. It's okay."

He pushed the pistol into my stomach. "*Zamovkny*."

"I don't know what you're saying."

He said something under his breath and let out a soft laugh, shuddering a little.

"I don't know what you're saying," I repeated, teeth gritted. "I don't know what's wrong."

He shoved himself up suddenly on his left arm. His face twisted in a grimace, but he kept the pistol dug under my breastbone while he swung his feet to the floor.

"I said *brekhukha*—liar." His voice was slow and thick. "And I said *zamovkny*, shut up, because I don't listen to liars like you." His left hand slipped around my waist, pulling me in against his knees. "And I said *moskalka* because I know you take their money. I know you are one of them."

"One of who?"

"KGB," he said.

Slowly, carefully, I placed my hand over his shaking, feverish one on my waist. How on earth could he be so sick so quickly? He had looked a little tired this morning, that was all. Those cuts on his hands? His ankle? But infection wouldn't set in like this, not even a tetanus infection—not this quickly, not this severely. It took days and sometimes weeks for tetanus symptoms to develop.

"Maksym." My mouth was dry as dust. "Maksym—I think maybe you're sick. I think maybe—"

He pulled me in close and tight, holding me in place against the pistol.

"Do you know what happened in the war?" He was trembling all over. His jaw was clenched tight; he was trying to keep his teeth from chattering. "To my family."

"Maksym—"

The muzzle of the pistol dug under my ribs. "Answer. Do you know?"

I shook my head mutely.

"Russians killed them. Not Germans. Did they tell you that? Russians killed them because my sister Anna, my older sister

Anna, she was a nurse in the underground. Ukrainian underground. So Russians came to the farm and shot all of them. My mother, my father, my sisters, my brothers. All of them. Russians did that. Russians did that to us." He let go of my waist all at once, shoving my hand off. He held up his left arm for me to see. "Look. This scar—do you know? I did it to myself. I had the number, the prisoner number. In Auschwitz, the Germans put the number there. I took it off myself. Do you know why? Because if you have the number, KGB send you to Gulag—to labor camps. They say you worked for the Germans. They say you are a collaborator." He spat weakly. "To hell with them. To hell with KGB."

"I'm not KGB."

"You take their money. You take their orders. You did this for them."

"I'm not KGB," I said softly. "I'm Shelby Blaine. I'm trying to help you."

"Telephone." His gun hand shook. "Bring the telephone."

"Maksym—"

He shoved the pistol under my ribs angrily, pushing me away. "Bring the telephone."

Numbly, I unwound the wire and brought him the handset from the kitchen. He held the pistol on me with one shaking hand while he brought out a scrap of paper from somewhere inside his coat—my scrap of paper, the one with Dad's office number—and took the receiver off the cradle.

"What are you doing?" I whispered.

"This number is police?"

"It's Dad's office—on base. Maksym, you can't call that number."

"You are doing it." He pushed the receiver toward me across the sofa. "Tell them you want Jones."

"Jones isn't there."

"*Zamovkny.*"

"Jones isn't there. I saw him this morning. He was going to Toronto." I swallowed. "Maksym—please listen to me. You're sick. You're not thinking straight."

His fingers trembled violently over the dial. He shook his head as if to clear away an irritatingly persistent gnat. "You are telling Jones. You are telling Jones you did this for them."

"Did what? I don't understand."

"This poison," he said.

As if on cue, he doubled up, leaned over his knees, and retched all over the carpet at my feet. I just barely managed to jump out of the way.

He must have been fighting it with everything he had, nothing held back in reserve, because that finished him. He curled up stiffly on his side against the sofa cushions when he was done. He didn't make a move to resist when I sat down beside him, the telephone between us, and leaned gingerly across him to ease the pistol from his fingers. He laid his head down and dug his face back into the crook of his left arm, shuddering silently.

Poison.

It didn't make any sense. He had been here in the house since yesterday noon. How could he have been poisoned? He hadn't touched anything except those eggs this morning, and I had eaten them too. He hadn't taken any coffee.

I reached out to touch his trembling, sweat-damp shoulder, panic curdling in the pit of my stomach. What if it *was* poison?

What was I supposed to do? I couldn't call a doctor for him; I couldn't take him to the hospital. I didn't know the first thing about poisons except what I had picked up from reading mystery novels, and the poisons always worked in those. That was the whole point. You didn't call in Hercule Poirot to save the victim. You called him in because the victim was dead.

"Maksym." I ran my hand over his shoulder lightly, hesitantly. "Did anything happen while I was gone? Did anybody come? Or maybe you ate something, or drank something—maybe it's just a food infection, or—"

"I know it is poison." His voice came up muffled and exhausted from the crook of his arm. "I know you did it. *Ya znayu.*"

I shook my head. I went on stroking his shoulder, trying to come off calmer than I felt. "Maksym—the only thing I could have poisoned was those eggs. That's the only thing you've eaten since you got here. And I ate them too. You saw me eat them."

"*Vchora.*" He turned his head onto his cheek, swallowing. "*Tabletky.*"

"What?"

"*Tabletky.* Tablets. Yesterday."

My chest went tight.

The aspirin. I had given him two of my aspirin tablets yesterday afternoon, when he was looking at the ceiling and pretending his ankle didn't hurt.

I snatched my handbag off the coffee table, dug furiously for the bottle—24 TABLETS BAYER ASPIRIN, FAST PAIN RELIEF—and poured every last tablet out onto the tabletop. Maksym watched, jaw clenched tight, face pale, while I sifted through them frantically. They all looked perfectly innocuous—eighteen little white tablets stamped with the Bayer trademark. Eighteen was right. I had bought this bottle at the Ramstein commissary just before we left. I had taken two tablets with a club soda on the MATS flight; I had taken two tablets after I slammed the phone on Agent Jones; I had given two tablets to Maksym. The bottle hadn't left my handbag in the meantime. It wasn't as if somebody had walked into the house and switched out the tablets while I was running my bath last night.

It couldn't be the aspirin.

Could it? Maybe he was allergic, violently allergic. You could be allergic to aspirin, couldn't you? Would it take this long for an allergic reaction to show?

I looked at the bottle in my hand. *Dose 1 or 2 tablets with water every 3 or 4 hours, 5 or 6 times daily as required. Important directions in leaflet.*

The leaflet, the leaflet—what had I done with it? I couldn't recall throwing it out. I had probably just shoved it into my handbag when I opened the bottle, not looking at it twice, because whoever needed directions for aspirin? But there would be warnings and emergency instructions in case of accidental ingestion, in case of overdose, in case of allergic reaction . . .

I tore through my handbag, yanking open zippers and clasps, dumping out lipsticks and compacts and tampons and old receipts. I unzipped my pocketbook and shook everything out onto the tabletop: three dollars and change left over after the cab fares, my base pass, Agent Jones's cabin key—

And the note.

It drifted down to land lightly among the aspirin tablets and spilled coins. I reached for it with numb, shaking fingers.

Nothing Agent Jones did was an accident.

Ethanol—ethyl alcohol, the antidote for ethylene glycol poisoning.

Agent Jones knew Maksym had been poisoned. He knew how.

And I was right. He knew Maksym was here.

THIRTEEN

I COULDN'T BELIEVE IT TOOK me this long to put it together.

I had stayed with Uncle Fred and Aunt Jean on the farm outside Columbus during the war. Dad enlisted in January 1942, and Mom started at the Curtiss-Wright aircraft plant that June. I had just turned five. Rather than foist me on the neighbors in our apartment building, she sent me out to the farm. One of the first things I remember, the very first day I got there, was Uncle Fred—4-F on account of an old break in his leg that hadn't ever set right—taking me around the barn at his slightly shuffled pace and showing me all the things I should keep away from: the tool wall, the combine, the bottles of rat killer and turpentine, the tins of antifreeze he kept for the truck radiator. He was particular about that antifreeze. He had a story about it. Kids do stupid stuff, he said. Did I want to know the stupidest thing he had ever done? When he was eleven years old, he swallowed a mouthful of antifreeze on a dare.

A mouthful—that was all. It didn't take much to kill you. Antifreeze was just about pure ethylene glycol, extremely toxic when ingested.

The story stuck with me just like the ones about rusty barbed wire and tetanus. I remembered his face in the barn that day. He had been dead serious. The scariest thing, he said, was how long it took to tell there was anything really wrong—more than twenty-four hours. He went most of that first day without any symptoms beyond a headache and some nausea, like being slightly hung over, and then he actually started feeling better—and the stuff was killing him inside the whole time. By the next morning, he was too weak to do anything but lean over the edge of his bed and vomit.

Twenty-four hours ago, Maksym had still been on base. Whoever had poisoned him had done it there.

Ethanol, Agent Jones's note said. They had saved Uncle Fred's life by pouring neat moonshine whiskey down his throat as an antidote. I don't know which surprised me more—that Uncle Fred had poisoned himself on a dare or that Grandma and Grandpa kept a bottle of moonshine in their cabinet.

I leaped up from the sofa and ran for the kitchen. We had whiskey. They hadn't given Dad the usual going-away party at Ramstein—it was so soon after the crash that I don't think the idea of a party ever crossed anybody's mind, which was ironic considering how Mom loved parties and would have been absolutely scandalized that Dad didn't get his—but all the officers in his squadron had pitched in for a bottle of Ambassador.

I sloshed three fingers of twenty-dollar Scotch into a tumbler and took it to Maksym.

He wouldn't take it.

He didn't say anything, but he turned his head away from the glass, burying his face back into the crook of his arm.

And that did it. That was the last straw. The CIA and FBI and police could all burst through the front door right now and shoot him, and I wouldn't even care—but so help me if he died like this. So help me if he died retching his guts out on my sofa because he was too stupid to take the damn antidote.

I leaned a knee on the sofa and hauled him up by his shirt collar.

He wasn't big, but he was solid muscle, and though he was too worn out to put up much of a fight, he was uncooperative. I had to put the whiskey on the coffee table and use both hands. I pulled him up so we were face-to-face—so close that he had to tip his head back a little to meet my eyes. The muscles in his throat fluttered as he swallowed.

"Listen to me." I held on tight to his collar. "Listen to me— you expected me to believe you. You expected me to trust you. 'It's just a mistake. It's not training. I'm not a spy.' You're the one with all those addresses and passwords. You're the one with ten thousand dollars and a pistol in your coat pockets. So you're going to trust me for a change, and you're going to drink this. It will help."

It will help. I think.

He looked up at me, swallowing against my fingers. He was blinking slowly, dazedly, as though he couldn't quite bring me into focus.

Finally, he spat out one word through clenched teeth. "Addresses."

I let go of his collar.

"Agent Jones says they found addresses in your bags. Addresses and codes and things for drops—that's what they called them. 'Intelligence drops.' That's why they're looking for you in Syracuse. They think you're passing intelligence to somebody in Syracuse." At least, Agent Kimball and the FBI thought so. I hadn't the faintest idea what Agent Jones thought.

Come to think of it, what was Agent Jones doing in Toronto? He wasn't following leads on Maksym if he knew Maksym was here.

"Who found them?" Maksym's voice was tight with effort. "Addresses. Who found them?"

"I don't know who found them. Agent Jones told me about them. He said they found them in your bags in your room on base."

"They put them there. They lied to Jones. I don't have addresses. I don't have codes. They put addresses there."

Could it be that simple? I supposed it could. If somebody on base could poison him, somebody on base could plant the stuff in his bags. Somebody on base could frame him. He hadn't told me about those addresses because he honestly hadn't known.

"I'll trust you if you trust me," I said.

He was silent for a moment, looking up at me, eyes dark, mouth tight. He exhaled softly—one weary, defeated breath. Then he suddenly leaned forward, snatched up the glass from the coffee table, and threw the whiskey back with two quick, grimacing swallows, squeezing his eyes shut.

I took the glass from him and poured another three fingers. "Again."

He finished off the second glass same as the first—in one swift, vengeful motion, as if he couldn't stand letting himself think about it for too long. When it was down, he sucked a shuddering breath and leaned over his knees, resting his face in one lacerated hand. His shoulders shook.

"I'm sorry," he said, "I'm sorry . . ."

I took the glass away from him before it slipped to the floor. I put Agent Jones's note in his hand.

He looked at it blankly through his fingers. Then he slid his hand down and held the scrap of paper on his palm. He traced one finger along the timetable; then he came to *ethanol*, penned in the margin. His lips moved faintly. It took me a moment to realize he was sounding it out to himself letter by letter. I didn't know whether his brain was that fogged or whether he just couldn't read English very well, the alphabet being different.

"Ethanol," I said. "Alcohol. It's an antidote for ethylene glycol poisoning. Don't ask me why it works, but it does."

"*Etylenhlikol*"—softly to himself.

"It's something they put in antifreeze." And in deicing fluid for planes, I imagined. It was a clever thing to use—practically untraceable on an air base, where there would be plenty of it sitting around, and no one would think twice about it. "It's poison. Somebody must have slipped it to you on base."

Maksym studied the slip of paper silently, looking at that word penned in neat small capitals. His chin came up; he held on to the paper tightly.

"This paper." He stumbled over the words as though he couldn't quite get his tongue to work. "This writing . . ."

"Agent Jones's—yes."

"Jones gave this to you?"

"This morning, in town. I think he knows you're here. I think he knows you've been poisoned. Maybe he found something out on base; I don't know." I hesitated. "I think he's trying to help you."

"Maybe because he is KGB—because we are both KGB."

I thought he was trying to make a joke, but he said it so flatly that I wasn't sure. "Maybe because he knows if somebody's trying to poison you, it means you're probably not KGB." And it meant somebody else *was*. That was why Agent Jones was treading so carefully, pulling all this sleight of hand with notes and motel keys hidden in bills. Somebody at Griffiss had poisoned Maksym. Agent Jones didn't know whom he could trust—besides me, apparently. I had no idea why he trusted me. I still had no idea what to make of that motel room.

"Do you remember?" I asked Maksym quietly. "It would have been yesterday morning, maybe Wednesday night—probably something you drank." Ethylene glycol was sugary sweet; Uncle Fred said antifreeze tasted something like Karo syrup. Stirred into sweetened coffee or tea, it might very well have gone unnoticed.

Slowly, very slowly, Maksym shook his head.

"What about at the party?"

"Jones said to drink nothing—always to drink nothing in places like that, public places." He gave me a ghost of a grin. "Why do you think I spilled the champagne?"

So Agent Jones had been anticipating poison. He had tried to safeguard Maksym against it. How many other cases like this had he seen? How many other would-be defectors had been murdered with poison? There must have been others. That Red agent in Jo's *Saturday Evening Post* had carried poison bullets in his cigarette-case gun.

"Then yesterday morning," I said to Maksym. "Did you drink anything with breakfast? Coffee? Tea? Cocoa? Anything sweet."

Another slow shake of the head. He was still clutching Agent Jones's note as though he were afraid to let it go, staring at it with that perplexed furrow dug between his brows.

"Well, let's get you cleaned up," I said. "Maybe it'll come back."

FOURTEEN

I GAVE HIM SOME OF Dad's clothes to put on after he showered. They were much too big for him—I had to cuff up the trousers before I could get at his ankle with the elastic bandage—but they would have to do until we found him new things. There wasn't any salvaging his ripped, reeking old suit. I couldn't walk into the cleaner's or the tailor's with it, not with his description posted on every bulletin board and storefront in upstate New York. His pistol and his money, ten thousand dollars in five slim, rubber-banded stacks of hundreds, went between layers of camisoles in my unmentionables drawer, along with that leaflet for the Ukrainian Canadian Relief Fund in Toronto. The suit went in the trash bin with a whispered apology: It was a Louis Roth, soft, sleek charcoal-gray shark-skin, and it deserved better. I wondered how Maksym had gotten it—whether he had bought it himself, not really comprehending how excessive it was, or whether it was standard procedure for the State Department to hand out $120 suits to valuable Eastern Bloc defectors as added incentive.

I thought it would be a good idea to get him out of the living room while I wrapped his ankle and dressed his hands—just in case, just so we wouldn't be left scrambling if somebody came to the door; he couldn't move very quickly. I hadn't reckoned with what it would be like having him in my bedroom. I hadn't had much time or space to worry about being shy around him. But with him in my room and the door shut and the silence in the house heavy around us, I was suddenly self-conscious and fidgety. All of a sudden, he wasn't a defector, or a test pilot, or a Red spy; he wasn't MAKSYM IVANOVYCH KOSTYSHYN, WANTED BY THE FBI.

All of a sudden, he was a boy in my bedroom.

Not just in my bedroom—in my bed.

It was so stupid to think about it. It was so wrong to think about it—and worse because I could guarantee you he wasn't thinking about it. He was sick and hurt and had a million other things on his mind; he probably couldn't care less right now about where he was or who I was or what the etiquette about girls' bedrooms was. But the closest a boy had ever come to my room was when Marty Miller waited at the foot of the stairs to pick me up for junior prom last year. Maksym was in my bed. It was impossible not to think about it.

I sat stiffly on the edge of the bed with the stuff from the drugstore spread out beside me on the coverlet. I wrapped up his bruised, swollen ankle; I dabbed at his hands with cotton balls soaked in antiseptic, taping Band-Aids over the worst of the cuts. I tried to cover up my nerves and the butterflies in my stomach by being cold and distant and fixing my face in a determined scowl, and he lay there so still and quiet, flat on his back, that I honestly thought he had fallen asleep. But he shifted when I twisted the dropper back into the antiseptic bottle and started gathering everything up.

"Maybe . . . this too," he said.

He hitched up the too-long hem of his shirt, Dad's shirt. His hands moved slowly and carefully, shaking a little.

The butterflies inside me quieted a bit. He was as nervous as I was.

The skin across his stomach was red and raw like skinned knees, ribboned in long, angry welts from the bottom of his rib cage to his navel, as if he had scraped his stomach across brick or cinder block. He must have done it when he climbed out of that window on base. And he was right; the scrapes needed antiseptic. But that wasn't what he was shy about, and it wasn't really what he was trying to show me.

Slowly, he moved his hand so I could see. There was an ugly gash of a scar running down the left side of his torso between waist and hip—and I knew at once that there was an awful, awful story behind that scar, and I knew he was trying to trust me with it and wasn't sure how.

I unscrewed the dropper and filled it again, calmly. I reached for another cotton ball.

"It's going to sting," I told him.

"It's okay," he said.

"How did it happen?"

And he knew I wasn't talking about those scrapes.

"In the war," he said as if by reflex. He paused, then added hesitantly, glancing up, "In the end of the war, when the Russians were coming. They were taking us out of the camp—the Germans. They were taking us to the train in Vodzislav. Fifty kilometers walking in the snow to Vodzislav. If you stopped walking, they would shoot. I stopped walking, so . . ." His hand moved over the scar again, trembling a little. "This is from when they took the bullet out—Red Cross. Russians found me still alive in the snow. They took me to the Red Cross hospital."

I leaned over him, head bent, dabbing at the scrapes as gently as I could—not that it made much difference. Merthiolate stings like the dickens. "How long were you there? In Auschwitz?"

"Not very long. From June. June to January—seven months only. Not very long. Some were there three years, four years."

"Is it because your family was in the underground?"

"No, it's—" He let out a breath. "Long story. It's because when the Germans were there, you had to have this document from the labor office, okay? This *Arbeitsbuch*, to show you had a job working for them. If you didn't have it, they could take you away to Germany—to work on farms in Germany. And it was supposed to be if you were twelve years or older. If you were twelve years old, you had to have it. And I didn't have it because that year I was ten. But they took me anyway. It didn't really matter to them if you were twelve. It didn't really matter about the document. They took you anyway if they wanted. That was in October, October 1943." He glanced up at me again, cautiously. "They sent me to work on a farm outside Heidelberg—do you know? Not very far from Ramstein."

"I know." I knew Heidelberg. It was just a little farther than Mannheim on the A6. I had been to the castle with Mom, and afterward we each got a *Studentenkuss* from one of the pastry shops and sat eating them and watching the rowing teams on the river. Heidelberg was a university town, not a factory town. It hadn't been targeted for bombing.

I remembered thinking in Heidelberg you could hardly tell there had been a war. I remembered liking it for that reason.

"I tried to run away," Maksym said. "As soon as I could, I

tried to run away. The first time, they found me pretty soon. The neighbor found me and took me back, and Lange—the farmer I worked for—he did this to me with . . . harness strap. Leather harness strap. He said it was better than what he should have done with me, so. I was lucky." He turned on his elbow, rolling up onto his side, just enough for me to see the white scars marching in rows across his back, disappearing under his shirt. He dropped flat on his back again. "The second time, I got farther. I got to Frankfurt. Police found me there. That's when they sent me to Auschwitz. That's what they were supposed to do if you tried to run away. That's what Lange meant." He lay still, watching me gather up the used cotton and twist the dropper back into the bottle. He hadn't even seemed to notice the sting.

"I never told anybody this," he said.

I set the bottle on the dresser. My throat was tight. "Nobody? Not even back home?"

"Okay—Zhenya knows. My wingman. He knows because sometimes in the night—sometimes I talk about it in the night, and he had to make me shut up. Because if KGB found out— not only about Auschwitz, but if they found out about the farm in Heidelberg, that I worked there—that I worked for a German . . ."

"They would send you to the labor camp."

"For collaborating. Yeah."

"This guy," I said, "Zhenya, your wingman—he was the one shooting at you when you defected? The one who shot up your plane?"

"They told him to shoot. It was orders. If he didn't shoot, KGB would shoot him."

"But he helped you keep the secret from them."

"It's different," Maksym said. "It's different to disobey an order like that."

It didn't seem much different to me. It was disobedience in either case, and I imagined the penalty was the same. But maybe there was some difference that he could see and I couldn't. Maybe it was different in some way that you couldn't understand unless you, too, had been under direct orders in the air.

"You didn't tell anybody here?" I asked. "In debriefing? The CIA or anybody?"

"Jones knows. Because I talk about it in the night, and he hears me sometimes. And this scar, the number . . ." He brushed his left arm absently against the sheets. "He was with them when they got to Flossenbürg camp—American Ninetieth Infantry. And some of the prisoners at Flossenbürg were there from Auschwitz, sent from Auschwitz, so they had the number. And he says he saw some of them doing this—taking it off like I did. So. He knows what the scar is." He hesitated. "But you're the first one I told. Not only that I talk about it in the night."

"You didn't need to tell me. You should have told them in debriefing. They need to know. They need to understand what you went through in the war."

"I want to tell you," he said.

He looked up at me. I looked down at him. The house was empty and silent; I could hear the *thump* of my heart stuck in my throat.

"I want to tell you," he repeated thickly, "in case I don't—"

I leaned over him and pressed my lips to his.

I wanted to stop him saying it, whatever it was—*In case I don't get another chance; in case I don't make it.* But mostly I wanted to kiss him.

He lay there stunned and silent and unmoving beneath me, holding on to the sheets in fistfuls—but then, just as I started to sit up, flushed and embarrassed, fumbling for an apology, he pushed up on an elbow and kissed my throat, soft as a whisper.

My breath hitched. I put a hand on his chest reflexively. He raised his head, leaning back on his elbows, studying me.

"Is it okay?" he asked.

I let out my breath carefully. "I don't know. Try it again."

He bent his head again obediently, brushing his lips across my neck.

"Yes—okay," I breathed, knotting my fingers in his too-big shirt, "definitely okay."

His hands slid around my waist, pulling me down, settling me cautiously against him, and I slipped my hands up under his shirt. My touch must have been cold on his bare skin. He sucked in a breath, tightening and shuddering a little. His head dropped back against the pillow.

I paused, looking down into his face. I could feel the beat of his heart under my palm. "Are you okay?"

"Yeah," he said.

He lay there looking up at me, his hands heavy on my waist. He was lying very still now, as though he were afraid he might startle me off if he twitched the wrong way. The muscles in his throat worked as he swallowed once, twice.

I stroked my fingertips along his chest and shoulders, heart in my throat, and dipped my head, lowering my mouth to him—shyly at first, then more certainly, feeling his mouth warm and tender and reassuringly patient against mine. I parted my lips, giving him permission, and he nudged in slowly and carefully with the tip of his tongue, searching lightly along my teeth, asking a wordless question. I opened to him fully in answer, and something yanked low and hard in the pit of my stomach as he slipped all the way in. He loosened beneath me, hands reaching up to caress my face, fingers tangling in my hair, and my breath caught in a shivering little gasp as his tongue found mine.

I had never kissed a boy like this. I had never wanted a boy like this—so badly I couldn't think or speak or breathe, so badly it made every part of me ache.

For a long moment after his mouth finally left mine, I just lay there breathless against him, holding on tight to his shoulders, feeling the thud of his heart against mine and the ragged rise and fall of his chest under my cheek. I had to make myself move. I leaned down and touched my lips very softly to the scar just above the sharp jut of his hip bone—the scar he had trusted to me.

Then, hands shaking, I reached over to the dresser for the merthiolate bottle. The first round wasn't going to do him much good; most of it was on the front of my blouse.

"I should probably do it again," I told him. "I'm sorry."

"Yeah," he rasped. "It's okay."

FIFTEEN

"QUESTION," I MURMURED TO HIM.

We were lying there in the half-light—just lying there on top of the bedclothes, warm and drowsy, not quite awake, not quite asleep. His left arm was around my shoulders, holding me safely against him. He was lying very still, breathing long and slow, as if he were one heartbeat away from nodding off—but every so often he would twitch a little, his breath catching, and his callused fingers would stroke out anxiously along my arm, as though he were reassuring himself that I was really there.

"Okay," he said.

"Why did you come over to my table?"

A puzzled pause. His fingers, stroking my arm, went still. "Your table?"

"At the dance—Wednesday night. What made you come over? The other CIA guy, Agent Mancuso—"

"Other CIA?"

"He was with Agent Jones this morning."

"I don't know another CIA."

"I think he came up from New York City. I think he came up on the train; I think Agent Jones picked him up at the station this morning. They must have sent him up to help."

"I think maybe they sent him up to watch Jones," Maksym said.

I turned this over in my head. It made sense. Agent Jones wasn't just treading carefully because he didn't know whom to trust; he was treading carefully because his CIA superiors didn't trust *him*. They must have thought it was too much of a coincidence—the way Maksym had escaped the dorm room, the way he had slipped his handcuffs and disarmed that MP all while Agent Jones was gone from the room. They had sent Agent Mancuso up here to be their watchdog.

All that rookie overenthusiasm in the car—all those spilled details of the investigation. *Fifty thousand dollars cash—a lot of dough.* And Agent Jones and I had both known perfectly well that it was only forty thousand. We had both known perfectly well where the other ten thousand was. That was the reason for Agent Jones's little sidelong look: He had been silently begging me not to fall for it, not to blurt out anything stupid about the money after I nearly threw the game away by mentioning Maksym's ankle.

All that time, I thought Agent Jones was the one trying to catch me out. Agent Mancuso had been trying to catch both of us out.

"He thinks you were trying to see if I was your contact," I said. "Agent Mancuso. He thinks that's why you came over. Or were you just trying to make a score?"

I couldn't see his face, but I knew his brow had dipped into that puzzled crease. "Make a score?"

"Trying to get a girl to dance with you or kiss you, or maybe . . . spend the night with you." My skin flushed hot all over. The words carried a lot more weight when you were, at the moment, literally in bed with a boy, even if he was being a perfect gentleman and you hadn't done anything more than a bit of kiss-and-cuddle. French kiss, admittedly.

"Flirting," he said.

"Sort of like flirting. A little more—calculated. Intentional. You know—you see a girl sitting alone at a table, and you make it into a game, getting her to go with you. Like scoring points in a game. Making a score."

"Making a score," he repeated gravely. "It's good to know." He was silent for a moment, then he said suddenly, "Because I brought the drink. The champagne. You thought I was making a score."

"I'm pretty sure Agent Jones thought so, too. I'm pretty sure that's why he was trying to frighten me off. Or does he let you bring girls home?"

"I wasn't making a score. I thought—because you came in with Colonel Blaine, and I didn't know you were Miss Blaine—"

"Shelby."

"Shelby," he agreed softly. His fingers brushed my arm, raising little goose bumps as they went. "I didn't know you were Shelby Blaine, and I thought maybe—"

"You thought I was his date?"

"I thought maybe. And you were alone. He left you there alone. And you looked—"

"Angry." I had been angry. I had been watching Agent Jones at the press table, thinking he was Maksym, and I had been simmering in resentment knowing that he was the reason we had to be here, the assignment that couldn't wait—knowing that he was more important to the Air Force than my dead mother.

"Sad," Maksym said quietly. "I thought all night you looked sad."

I swallowed against his chest. My throat was knotted tight. "So you were watching me all night."

"Maybe I was trying a little bit to make a score."

He was joking; I knew he was joking. And I had put him up to it. But something went cold and hard inside me just the same. He hadn't answered that question about taking girls home.

I didn't even care how many other girls he had taken home. But I hated the thought—even as a joke, even if he didn't mean it—that he had looked at me that night, sitting alone and miserable and vulnerable at my empty table, and seen an easy score.

"My mom died a month ago," I said shortly. "On Wednesday it was exactly a month ago—June sixth."

His fingers went still.

"It was in Germany. On the autobahn outside Mannheim—right after she dropped me off at school. The roads were wet. She lost control of the car. They said it was instantaneous; she wouldn't have felt anything. She wouldn't have had time to feel anything. But they always say that, don't they? 'It was instantaneous.' They always tell you that, no matter if it's true."

I caught my breath. I hadn't cried one drop for her—not even at Ramstein, not even the morning it happened. Dad hadn't cried, so I hadn't cried. If he could be strong, I could be strong. But I was afraid I was going to start crying now.

Maksym's callused hand brushed over my hair, cupping my head against his chest.

"It's okay," he said. "It's okay. It's good to cry."

"Do you?"

He was silent for a moment. I felt him exhale softly beneath me.

"In the night," he said. "Sometimes in the night. Jones knows."

"Does he have to do this for you?" I asked sourly. "Hold you and tell you everything's okay?"

"Not exactly this." His voice was dry. "He gives me whiskey. He says we can talk about it if I want. He says maybe it helps to talk about it. But I don't talk about it." His fingers stroked carefully through my hair. "Only to you."

I pushed myself up from him all at once, shrugging his arm off. What was I thinking? I couldn't cry in front of this boy. He had lain here dry-eyed and matter-of-fact and unblinking, telling me every god-awful thing done to him in Heidelberg, in Auschwitz, showing me each horrible scar, each deliberate cruelty. And I was going to pieces because my mother had crashed her car on the autobahn while making a shopping trip. She had probably been speeding anyway. She always did.

I felt the corners of my eyes quickly to make sure there weren't any tears, careful not to smudge my mascara, and swung my legs over the edge of the bed so I could slip my pumps back on.

"I'm going up to base," I said tightly. "We need to tell Dad you're here."

Maksym went very still.

"He needs to know." I yanked sharply at one T-strap after the other. "If there's a KGB agent on base, intelligence needs to know."

"I think maybe . . ." His voice was slow and careful. He reached for me, fingers tracing lightly down my back. His hand slipped around my waist. "Maybe we can wait for Jones, okay? Come back to bed."

"Agent Jones didn't say when he would be back. He didn't say what he was doing."

"I think maybe Colonel Blaine will still think I am KGB." He pulled at me ever so gently. "Come back to bed, Shelby. We can wait."

For a moment, I wavered. His hand was so warm and strong on my waist, and just for a moment I wanted to be persuaded. I wanted it so badly. I wanted to slip back under his arm and let him pull me down close and tight against him and let the tears finally come and let him kiss them away.

But I didn't. My grief was mine; he had plenty of his own.

I tugged away from him.

"We can prove you're not KGB. We can prove somebody on base was trying to kill you." I went around the bed to get a fresh blouse from the closet. I unbuttoned and changed and rebuttoned behind the closet door, safely out of his sight—though there was a rebellious part of me imagining, just for a moment, that his fingers were the ones undoing each button one after the other, pulling the blouse open and slipping it off my shoulders; and then of course my fingers wouldn't cooperate. I shut my eyes, drawing a careful breath. "And you need to be in the hospital. We don't know how much damage that stuff did to you."

"I feel okay now. Only tired. A little tired."

I emerged from the closet to find that he had turned politely away, shifting onto his side, his back to me. "Maksym."

"I think maybe we can wait for Jones," he said doggedly to the far wall. "I think it's better to wait."

"Maksym, he could be days. We can't wait for him. Look—he gave me that note because he wanted to make sure you got treatment. He trusted me to make sure you got treatment. I'll bet anything he wasn't just expecting me to pour some whiskey down your throat and pretend everything was okay. You need X-rays. You need blood work. You need actual medicine."

"Jones gave you the note," Maksym said quietly. "He didn't give Colonel Blaine the note."

"He must have known I would pass it along. For all I know, he meant for me to pass it along."

"Maybe we can telephone Jones in Toronto."

"Maybe you can trust me," I snapped.

He was silent, looking at the wall.

I dug in my handbag and opened my pocketbook to make sure I had put my base pass back in. "Look," I said, "I'm not going to talk to anybody but Dad. But he needs to know. They need to know they're going after the wrong guy."

"Don't," he said.

He rolled back over to face me, leaning on his elbow, moving his right arm over the coverlet to show me the pistol in his hand. He had slipped it from the dresser while I was out of sight behind the closet door.

"Colonel Blaine says they will make a prisoner exchange in Moscow." He wasn't aiming at me this time, just resting the pistol lightly atop the bedclothes—making sure I knew it was there. "They'll send me back," he said. "I can't go back."

I stood very still, one hand on the doorknob. "They're not going to send you back. They won't send you back if you don't want to go." *Would they?*

"Colonel Blaine will send me back. He says I am lying to them."

"Maksym, we can prove you're not lying. They'll test your blood for toxin levels—it's called a toxicology report. They can probably tell us exactly when it happened. They can tell us who did it."

"But I did lie," he said.

"What?"

"I did lie to them. CIA, FBI. Danish intelligence. All of them. Colonel Blaine is right. He has the photos. He knows I lied."

"The photos—"

"I didn't sabotage the plane. I didn't put a bomb. He's wrong about that. It was an accident only. There was . . . malfunction. Electrical malfunction. I lost control. I had to eject. I had to ditch the plane. A boat picked me up in the water, Danish boat. They took me to Bornholm, and I was afraid—because Denmark is NATO, okay? I was afraid maybe they would give me as a prisoner to the British, to the Americans. So I lied. I said I was Ukrainian. I said I was trying to defect. I said Zhenya shot me down because I was trying to defect. I didn't know they would be able to salvage the plane. I didn't know they would take photos." He swallowed.

"I'm not KGB," he said. "I'm not a spy. But I wasn't trying to defect."

"So is it all just lies?" I felt winded and slightly sick—that feeling you get when the plane hits an air current and your stomach plummets away. "Everything you just told me—your family in the Ukrainian underground, Auschwitz—"

"Auschwitz isn't a lie." There was a rough edge to his voice.

"But your family?"

He hesitated.

"From Leningrad. They died in the siege—my parents. They sent me out of the city when the Germans were coming. They sent me to cousins in Kalinin. For two years I was in Kalinin. That's where the Germans took me."

"You're Russian."

"I was afraid to tell them. All this time, I've been lying in the debriefings, making up a story that Zhenya shot me down, because I was afraid to tell them I am Russian. I was afraid to tell them I wasn't trying to defect."

He was watching my face, looking for my reaction—looking to see whether I was angry. Was I? I didn't know whether I was. Those scars weren't lies. And what if he had told the truth on Bornholm—that it was only an accident, not a daring flight to freedom? What would we have done with him? What were Red pilots told to expect if they were downed in NATO airspace?

If their propaganda painted us anything like the way ours painted them, he might very well have been expecting a show trial and a savage execution.

So he had lied.

He had lied his way right into political asylum and American citizenship and a Louis Roth sharkskin suit and a meeting with President Eisenhower and fifty thousand dollars of State Department money.

No wonder he was afraid to go back. He had shown me that scar on his arm; he had told me what the KGB did with so-called traitors and collaborators. They wouldn't believe that ditched plane had been an accident, not now. They would send him to a labor camp—or they would shoot him.

My silence seemed to reassure him. He loosened just a little.

"Please," he said quietly. "Please don't go to Colonel Blaine."

"I've got to." I squared my shoulders. "The KGB is treating you as a defector whether you meant it or not. There's a KGB agent at Griffiss with orders to kill you." And evidently with a high-level security clearance too. Whoever they were, they had managed to get close enough to Maksym to poison him without raising Dad's suspicions or Agent Jones's. "Dad needs to know. And you need the hospital. I'm done playing spies, all right?"

"Don't, Shelby." His voice was tight.

"Then shoot me," I said.

He lay there leaning silently on his elbow, looking at me. I tried not to look at the pistol on the bedclothes; I tried to keep my eyes on his. But I could see it sidelong. I could see his hand on it, tensed and ready—fingers curled around the grip, forefinger resting lightly on the trigger.

He slid his finger from the trigger all at once. He dropped flat against the pillow, exhaling softly.

"Tell him I made you do it," he said to the ceiling. "You only helped me because I made you do it, okay? Because of this." He indicated the pistol with a twitch of his hand.

"I'm going to tell him the truth," I said. "One of us should."

SIXTEEN

DAD'S OFFICE WAS IN THE headquarters of the Air Development Center, just off the airfield apron; he had pointed it out to me from the rental car on Tuesday morning. The letter board directory on the wall in the lobby said 2ND FLOOR— INTEL ADMIN.

I knew where to go; I just couldn't get there.

"I need to talk to Colonel Blaine," I told the secretary at the front desk. "Rob Blaine. He's my dad. It's important."

She pushed her smart cat's-eye glasses back up her nose with one fingertip and slid my base pass back to me without looking at it. "You need a security clearance to be in here, Miss Blaine."

"Then could you please phone him?"

"Not for personal business—not during duty hours." Her auburn head, sleek and neat in a French twist, bent back disinterestedly over her steno pad. "I can take a message."

"Please do."

"I meant I can take down a message," she clarified, not raising her head. She lifted a world-weary hand toward the mail slots on the wall over her shoulder.

"Just tell me which window is his. I'll go outside and throw pebbles," I snapped.

It wasn't her fault. Rules were rules. But I wanted to reach across the desk and shake her by her collar tabs. Dad was right up the stairs. I could see the second-floor landing from here. He would probably hear me if I raised my voice a little more. The security officer at the foot of the stairs was already looking my way.

I closed my eyes.

"Please—I just need to talk to him. It's very important."

Her lips pursed. She rapped her nails—perfect Air Force blue to match her uniform jacket—once across the desktop, then she leaned over to snatch up her telephone receiver. She spun the dial smoothly with a fingertip.

"Yes—hello, Lieutenant. Could you let me know when the colonel is out of his briefing?" She looked up at me, raising her eyebrows and jutting out her chin as if to make sure I had caught the favor: Dad wasn't in his office. She just wasn't allowed to tell me directly.

"Thank you," I murmured, chastened.

"Right," she said into the receiver. "Thank you, Lieutenant." She laid the phone back down and pointed with the end of her pen. "Out the door; take a left on the parkway; go past depot supply. Base library's on the right. You don't need a security clearance to be in there. And they've got air-conditioning. You can wait there. I'll make sure the colonel knows where you are."

So here I was, sitting at one of the reading tables among the library stacks, drumming one foot, watching the hands of the wall clock drag themselves slowly forward: 3:20—3:27—3:32.

In hindsight, I should have called Dad's number before I came—not that I would dare spill anything over the phone. I knew enough about telephone taps and clandestine surveillance; they had been plenty in the news and in dinner conversations these past few years, thanks to Senator McCarthy and his Red witch hunts. It was entirely possible that a KGB agent would think to tap the base lines. But I could at least have checked whether Dad would be in his office.

Three forty. Maksym had been alone in the house for nearly an hour. He said he was tired, only tired, but I knew he was lying. I knew he felt worse than he was letting on. I had felt the fever burning him up. I should have made him take more aspirin. I should have made him drink more water. Should I have given him more whiskey? I couldn't imagine they had given eleven-year-old Uncle Fred much more than two three-finger shots at once—you would have to start worrying about alcohol poisoning—but maybe they had given him more at intervals.

I shouldn't have left him.

I should just go home. Dad would probably be home by six or so anyway.

Unless he decided to spend the night on base again.

I needed to give my fidgeting hands something to do. Somebody had left a bunch of reference books spilled over the tabletop, scattered every which way. Absently, I started pulling them together, stacking them up. One was the Rand McNally *Encyclopedic World Atlas*; another was Margaret Mann's *Europe: A Modern Geography*. That one gave me pause. I flipped it open, fanning the pages under my fingers, looking over the chapter headings—slowly and rather aimlessly at first, then with more intention, picking up the pace: GENERAL INTRODUCTION TO

We knew about Leningrad, of course. Even on the Ohio home front, we heard about Leningrad—that proud, indomitable city, the jewel of Russian culture, holding out desperately against the German onslaught, enduring two and a half terrible but epic years of blockade. There had been poetic write-ups and glossy photo essays in *Time* and *Life* and *The New Yorker*; in fact Mom had kept the *Time* feature about the NBC Orchestra premiere of Shostakovich's Seventh Symphony, written during the siege. Mom had loved Shostakovich, Stravinsky, Prokofiev, all the strange modernist composers. She had loved them defiantly—though after the war, when it started being questionable to like modernists and especially Russian ones, she would slip the records discreetly behind Bing Crosby whenever we had company over.

The world had changed so quickly. I couldn't imagine *Time* or *Life* printing anything about the heroic glory of Leningrad now. Everything was backward; everything was wrong. Russia was the enemy. The Germans were our allies. Mom's records had all gone in donations to the base charities back at Ramstein.

Europe: A Modern Geography mostly avoided anything about the war, like papering over a gaping hole in the wall. There was a good deal more about Leningrad's historic waterways and trade links than about the siege—pages and pages on the extensive Volga canal system that linked Leningrad to inland cities like Yaroslavl, Novgorod, Kalinin (formerly Tver)—

And then, stuck in like an afterthought: *Kalinin, roughly one hundred miles north of Moscow, was liberated after two months of*

German occupation in December 1941—the first major Russian city to be retaken by the Red Army.

Maksym said he had been with cousins in Kalinin for two years after the siege of Leningrad began—that would have been in September 1941; I remembered the date very clearly. But Kalinin had been liberated from the Germans in December of that year.

There was no way the Germans had taken ten-year-old Maksym in Kalinin in October 1943.

Maybe the Germans had recaptured Kalinin at some point, and Margaret Mann just hadn't found that as interesting to include. Maybe there were lots of Kalinins. Maybe "Kalinin" was like "Washington" in the US. Wasn't there a Washington in every state? Maybe there were Kalinins all over Russia, and Maksym hadn't bothered to specify which because I wouldn't know the difference anyway.

That had to be it. Didn't it?

Except there was only one Kalinin in Rand McNally's *Encyclopedic World Atlas.*

I shoved the books away and scraped my chair back. Wiretapping be damned. I hadn't been angry earlier, but I was now. Maksym had been lying to me through his teeth.

"I need Toronto directory assistance," I told the long-distance operator from the library's ancient public phone.

"Daytime rate to Toronto is one dollar per two minutes."

I dug for my pocketbook, counting out the coins hurriedly. Dad was going to kill me. "That's fine."

"Ready with Toronto."

The Toronto operator came on the line. "Name, please?"

I leaned my elbows on the table, ducking my head down. I was alone in the phone room with the door shut, but I still felt as if I were drawing attention—as if I were being watched. "I was wondering if you could help me with the names of some of the hotels there—some of the hotels where an airline passenger might be staying? I'm trying to reach someone who's traveling."

"Well—there's the airport hotel, of course—but if they're in the city for any length of time . . . there's the Royal York on Front Street and the Sheraton on King Street. The Royal York is just across the street from the station—Union Station."

"Could you put me through to the Royal York?"

"Yes—hold, please."

There was a moment's silence, then—

"Royal York Toronto." The voice was a man's voice, slightly harried. I could hear a dull roar of laughter and chatter in the background.

I swallowed; my mouth was dry. "Yes—I'm looking for a guest there."

"The name, madam?"

I hesitated. I had no idea what Agent Jones's first name was, and it seemed incredibly suspect to be trying to reach the hotel room of somebody whose name I didn't even know.

"Mancuso," I said, "Dean Mancuso."

"There's no one under that name in the register, madam."

I shut my eyes. "Could you tell me if there's a Jones—a Mr. Jones? I don't know his first name."

"No, madam."

"You can't tell me?"

"I don't have a Mr. Jones, madam."

My heart sank. "Oh. Well, thank you very—"

"Yes—good day, madam," he said, and hung up.

I used up another two dollars calling up the King Edward Sheraton and the Malton Airport hotel. There was neither Mancuso nor Jones at the Sheraton. There *was* a Jones at the airport hotel, but a woman. I hung up the receiver after I got off the line at the airport hotel. It was useless. I couldn't call every single hotel in Toronto and ask to speak with every single Jones just in case.

For the first time, I wondered whether that was his real name. It was an incredibly convenient name for a CIA officer.

Maybe if I called the airport? If I called the airport taxi stand? Agent Jones and Agent Mancuso might have taken a cab from the airport to wherever they were going; the driver might remember . . .

Wait.

I picked up the receiver again, and the long-distance operator put me back through to Toronto directory assistance.

"Name, please?"

"The Ukrainian Canadian Relief Fund." My heart had jumped up to my throat. "Do you have a number for the Ukrainian Canadian Relief Fund?"

A stretch of silence.

"Yes, ma'am. I've got that number. Would you like me to connect you?"

"Yes," I whispered.

"I'm sorry, ma'am?"

"Yes."

"Hold, please."

And then, before I had a chance for second thoughts—
"UCRF Toronto office; good afternoon. This is Lydia."

I sat there frozen, gaping into the receiver.

"Hello? *Allo? Tse Ukrayins'ko*—"

"Yes—hello." I drew a breath, willing my voice not to shake. "I'm looking for Dean Mancuso."

"I'm sorry—again, please?"

"I'm looking for Mr. Dean Mancuso. I'm, um . . ." Why hadn't I come up with a cover story first? "His secretary. I'm his secretary. Shelby Blaine. I believe he had an appointment there today. I've been trying to reach him."

"The name is Mancuso?"

"Yes, Dean Mancuso. With the, um—the Ukrainian American Relief Fund." I had no idea whether there was such a thing. What was I supposed to say—"I'm looking for Dean Mancuso, the CIA officer"?

"I'm afraid there's been a mix-up. I don't have him on my appointment list." She sounded apologetic, not suspicious.

"He's with a colleague, a Mr. Jones." I slipped the phone cord around my fingers. "I don't know his first name; I'm sorry."

"Let me check . . ." A murmur of muffled voices in the background; she had put her hand over the speaker. "I don't think they've been in today, Miss Blaine. I'm sorry. I can schedule another appointment for Monday if you'd like. What is this in reference to?"

"Actually . . . actually, maybe you can help—us."

"Yes, Miss Blaine?"

I dug hastily in my purse with my free hand, fumbling my way around my pocketbook and the jumble of things I had shoved indiscriminately back in. I withdrew Maksym's crumpled flyer and smoothed it out with sweating, shaking fingers.

"Yes—we're looking for information about a Ukrainian

family. The Kostyshyns, from Kulikov. Any information at all that you might have—any records, any documents—"

"Kulikov," she repeated. "Kulikov—L'viv Province?"

"Yes." I had no idea. "Yes, I think so."

"Yes, it's so difficult, that area—all the resettlements. Here, let me put you through to one of our executive directors—Mr. Romaniuk. He's from L'viv. He handles most of the cases from that region. Mr. Kyrylo Romaniuk."

"Thank you."

A pause.

"I'm so sorry, Miss Blaine. I forgot he was out of the office today. Let me give you his home number."

"Oh, no, please, you don't have to—"

"No, no, it's all right—he asked me to forward his calls. His wife had to go out of town unexpectedly, so he's home today; that's all. I just forgot. It's quite all right. Have you got a pen?"

The librarian changed out my last dollar bill for more quarters, and I stood chewing nervously on my bottom lip while the long-distance operator put the call through to EMpire 3–5425, Toronto. This was such a mistake. I shouldn't have called. I could bluff my way past poor Lydia, who probably just wanted to be home at four o'clock on a Friday afternoon, but this guy was an executive director. I bet he could tell I didn't have anything to do with some "Ukrainian American Relief Fund."

"Hello! Mykola Kobryn speaking."

Another moment of gaping. The voice on the other end of the line was young—a kid's voice.

"Oh, I—I think I must have gotten the wrong number,

sorry. I'm trying to reach a Mr. Roman . . ." Why hadn't I written the name down too? "Roman something."

"Romaniuk. That's my dad."

"Oh." I wasn't sure whether to be relieved. I was half hoping it *was* the wrong number. "Is he—"

Then I froze.

"Kobryn. You said your name is Kobryn."

"Yeah. I'm Mykola. Kyrylo's my dad. We just have different names because he's really my stepdad."

He explained this all perfectly levelly—as if he were reciting it, as if he were used to doing it—but I fumbled for an apology just the same.

"No—I'm sorry, I just meant—" How on earth was I supposed to explain to some kid that I had stumbled across the name *Kobryn* in a motel in upstate New York this morning? "Never mind. Is he there? Your dad?"

"Yeah. Do you want to talk to him?"

"Yes. Please."

"Okay. Hang on just a second."

There was a muffled bump as he laid the receiver down, then a sudden rustle as he picked it back up again.

"With whom am I speaking?"

"I'm sorry?"

"I'm supposed to say, 'With whom am I speaking.' I forgot."

"Oh—you're speaking to Shelby. Shelby Blaine."

"Okay," he said, and set the phone down again; and a moment later—"Dad? Hey, Dad?" and then the *thump, thump, thump* of his footsteps racing upstairs, fading out of earshot.

I waited, heart caught in my throat—listening to the silence, praying my quarters would last. It seemed ages before another set of footsteps came distantly *thump, thump, thump*-ing down the stairs.

Another voice came on the line—a man's voice this time.

"This is Kyrylo Romaniuk. Is something wrong, Miss Blaine?"

He sounded so much like Maksym—a slightly older, slightly less accented Maksym—that for a second I didn't notice how odd a greeting it was.

"H-hello, Mr. Romaniuk." I adjusted my grip on the receiver; my hands were slippery. "I'm sorry to bother you. Lydia gave me your number—at the UCRF—"

"Are you at home?"

"I'm sorry?"

"Are you calling from your home phone, Miss Blaine?"

"No—no, from a public phone, a pay phone." Was he afraid I was going to reverse the charges? "I'm not calling collect, if that's what you mean."

He hissed a soft breath. I thought it was a laugh, but over the wires I wasn't sure. "That's all right, Miss Blaine. A public phone is good. Are you at the motel, then?"

I nearly dropped the receiver. "What?"

"Agent Jones said he gave you the key."

"Y-yes—yes, he did. I've got it." My tongue wouldn't cooperate. "But I'm not at the motel. I'm on base. I'm—"

"Base?" His voice sharpened. "Is Maks with you now?"

I hardly dared breathe. The words stumbled out in a whisper. "He told you? Agent Jones told you?"

Silence on the other end. And then—

"I think maybe he told us more than he told you, Miss Blaine. I'm Maksym's brother-in-law."

SEVENTEEN

THE LINE WENT DEAD.

I was out of time.

I was out of quarters.

I toggled the line switch uselessly. The long-distance operator's voice crackled in my ear.

"Do you wish to continue the call?"

"Yes, just a second . . ." I held the receiver between my cheek and shoulder while I turned my pocketbook upside down and shook it out hastily. A shower of small change scattered all over the phone table—pennies and nickels and dimes rolling every which way among the yellow-page directories. I gathered them together as quickly as I could, fingers trembling.

"Hello, ma'am?"

"Just give me a second . . ." Twenty, twenty-five, thirty, thirty-three—

Thirty-seven cents, plus a few leftover deutsche mark coins I had forgotten to exchange at the Finance Office.

"Would you like to reverse the charges?" the operator asked.

"Shel?"

Dad was standing in the phone room doorway, cap tucked under his arm, briefcase in hand.

"I—I'll call back," I managed.

My hands shook as I hung up the receiver. I felt off-kilter, as if the floor had been yanked suddenly from under my feet. Had Maksym known this whole time that he had a brother-in-law in Toronto? He must have known. Agent Jones apparently knew. And the brother-in-law knew who I was. The brother-in-law assumed I knew who he was.

Dad shut the door. "Who was that?"

I hesitated. I couldn't just blurt it out—*Oh, that was Maksym's brother-in-law, and by the way, Maksym is in my bedroom right now.* If I started like that, he wouldn't hear any of the rest of it.

"The seamstress's," I said softly. "I was trying to see about getting that dress fitted—the new dress. I want to wear it to Mom's service."

He drew up another chair. "The seamstress is in Toronto?"

The scrap of notepaper I had scribbled Mr. Romaniuk's number on was there on the table. He had seen the exchange code.

"She's a specialized seamstress," I said. "She works with that kind of silk shantung. They couldn't do it here in Rome."

He tossed his cap down and leaned his briefcase against the table leg. I couldn't tell whether he bought it. "Well, it's good you came up," he said. "I need to talk to you."

Calmly, I picked up Mr. Romaniuk's scrap of paper, folded it into a tiny square, and dropped it into my purse. I started brushing coins carefully off the table into my palm, tipping them back into my pocketbook. "Okay."

"I've got to go down to Washington," he said.

My hand slipped. Coins bounced across the floor. "What?"

"Just for a couple of days. I think."

159

"When?"

He looked away. "Now. I'm leaving now. I was going to call you."

"Now as in right now."

"Plane's on the tarmac. I'm sorry, Shel. Something came up, and they need me to go. Here . . ." He took his wallet from his lining pocket and slid a ten-dollar bill over to me. "In case you need some cash."

"Is this because of the Russian? Is this because they still haven't found him?"

He tucked his wallet back inside his coat. "I'll call you as soon as I'm in, all right? I'm not sure where they're putting me up yet, so—"

"I know where he is."

"What?"

"I know where the Russian is," I said.

Dad went very still, hand outstretched to his cap.

"He came to the house," I said. "I've been hiding him at the house. He's been there since yesterday."

A sudden flurry of footsteps, a quick knock at the doorway. The librarian poked her head in.

"Closing in five minutes, Colonel," she murmured, and flitted away again.

It was surreal—that moment of sheer normalness coming on the heels of my confession. Despite everything, it was still four thirty on a Friday afternoon in July in Rome, New York, and the library was closing.

I wanted to laugh. But I didn't dare laugh.

Slowly, very slowly, Dad pulled his cap across the table. He dipped his head and put it on. His face was dead blank, as if that switch had been shut off inside him.

"Have you told anyone else?"

"Agent Jones knows. He's been helping me."

His chin came up a little. "Jones."

"He's been helping me," I repeated tightly. "Or I've been helping him. I think he's the one who helped Maksym get off base in the first place." At least, I thought he had made it possible. He had taught Maksym how to slip handcuffs. He had given himself an excuse not to be in the room.

It occurred to me that I had said Maksym's name.

I hadn't meant to say his name. He was only That Russian. His name didn't matter. *He* didn't matter, per se. It was the principle of the thing. I was helping him because it was the objectively right thing to do. Otherwise, I was just little Miss Blaine who had fallen for the Soviet spy. Even Dad would think so—especially if he found out how I had spent my afternoon.

But Dad, who caught everything, didn't catch my mistake this time.

He leaned his elbows on the table, resting his head in his hands, kneading his temples with his blunt, callused fingertips. His voice came out muffled and exhausted between his palms.

"Jones wasn't helping you, Shel. They knew Kostyshyn was a KGB operative. The agency knew before they sent him to us. They knew the defection was fake."

"He isn't KGB."

"They wanted to see if they could use him to uncover any more of a network—double agents, other operatives. That's why Jones let him go off base. They wanted to see what he would do. They wanted to see where he would go for help, who he would try to contact—"

"He isn't KGB. Dad, if you send him back, they'll kill him."

Dad slid his hands down all at once. He leaned below the edge of the table to open his briefcase. He brought out a manila folder, turned it over, and laid it open on the table in front of me. There was a stack of full-page photographs of a silver-sleek Soviet jet fighter.

"His MiG," Dad said.

I sat there looking at those photos. There were four or five photos of the whole thing—what was left of it after the crash—taken from different angles. One wingtip and the tail fin were sheared cleanly away. That must have happened when it hit the water, cartwheeling across the surface before it went under; water is as hard as concrete when you hit it at hundreds of miles an hour. And of course the canopy had ripped away when Maksym ejected. But the fuselage was mostly intact. There were photos and photos of the fuselage and cockpit and controls, blown up close to show detail. The instrument panel was a burned-out, mangled shell—switches blown, gauges shattered, wires spilled loose and tangled like yarn. The bare metal innards of the cockpit were streaked black with charring.

"He destroyed as much of it as he could," Dad said. "He had to give us the MiG to sell the defection. But he made sure we weren't going to be able to do anything with the flight system."

"He wasn't trying to defect." I pushed the folder away. "It was just an accident—an electrical malfunction of some sort. He wasn't trying to defect. He lied to you because he was afraid."

"I know he did," Dad said. "I'm asking you to consider the possibility that he was doing the same to you."

"Dad, he's been poisoned." I dropped my hands to my lap. I didn't want him to see them shaking. "That's what I came to tell you. Somebody on base poisoned him. Somebody on base was trying to kill him." I dug my fingernails into my palms. "I think the KGB has an agent at Griffiss with orders to kill him."

Slowly, Dad closed the folder and put it away in his briefcase.

"He told you he'd been poisoned?"

"He didn't have to tell me. He was puking all over the living room."

Dad was silent.

"You think I'm lying." My throat was tight with sudden fury. "You think I'm lying for him—covering for him."

"I think he needed you to trust him."

"So he poisoned himself?"

"I think a KGB agent might if he wanted you to trust him."

I scraped my chair back, fumbling at the strap of my handbag. "I've got to go."

Dad dug his fingers into his eyelids. "Wait, Shelby."

"I've got to go. He's running a fever."

"Wait."

"You don't have to believe me. Agent Jones does."

Dad slammed one palm flat on the tabletop—so sharply that I jumped. I had never seen him snap like that.

He looked up at me. His face was blank; his voice was quiet.

He said, "City police found Kostyshyn about an hour ago."

"What?"

"One of the patrol cars picked him up on the state route north of town. They turned him over to Jones—"

"Agent Jones is in Toronto."

"His flight came in at fifteen hundred. He took the call; Kimball's still in Syracuse." Dad shrugged a little. "Apparently—while he was bringing him in—apparently, Kostyshyn tried to make a break—"

"No."

"Jones shot him," Dad said. "That's what I'm trying to tell you, Shel. He's dead. Jones was never helping you."

EIGHTEEN

DAD DROVE ME TO THE house, I think.

I don't remember exactly. Everything was blurred and jumbled. Somehow, we were at the house, and he was waiting in the living room while I packed an overnight bag. He must have gotten clearance to take me with him on the flight to Washington; I had a vague memory of his making murmured arrangements with somebody over a telephone. I don't remember when or where that was—whether he phoned somebody right there from the library, or whether we stopped somewhere on the way to the house, or whether I made that phone call up, and he was just expecting that they would give me a clearance because he was Colonel Blaine and he told them to. I don't remember. I don't know.

I do remember opening up my dresser in my empty bedroom and finding Maksym's State Department money still folded carefully among my camisoles—all ten thousand dollars of it, five neat rubber-banded stacks. I took it all out and put it on the bed and counted through each stack just to be sure.

He had taken the pistol and the leaflet for the Ukrainian Canadian Relief Fund and the New York State road map I bought for him this morning at the Esso station. He had been careful not to leave any other traces. His towel was gone from the hall bathroom; the merthiolate bottle had vanished from the top of the dresser. My bed was made up.

But he had left the money.

At first, I thought maybe he had just forgotten. I wasn't sure it had ever really sunk in for him—how much money he was carrying around in that suit coat. The Soviet ruble was weak against the dollar; ten thousand rubles probably didn't amount to all that much. Maybe in his mind ten thousand dollars was something you might understandably forget in a dresser drawer.

But I was wrong. He hadn't forgotten. He had left a note for me, folded neatly under the rubber band on one of the stacks.

A letter, really—four pages from the little notepad I had been keeping in the kitchen for grocery lists, printed over front and back in careful, rather uncertain Latin letters. He had, I thought, written it out for himself in Russian first, then ripped those pages out. You could see the faint little traces of the characters etched into the paper.

Dear Shelby,

I want to tell you the truth.

Do you remember about my wingman, Zhenya? His name is Evgeny Sergeyevich Andreyev. Zhenya is his nickname. He is Russian, from Leningrad. When I told you the story about Leningrad, that my parents died in the siege but I lived because they sent me to cousins in Kalinin, I was telling you Zhenya's story.

I am not Russian. I am Ukrainian.

I will tell you what I remember. It's hard to remember every-thing now because I was only ten years old the last time I saw my family, in October 1943, and twelve years old the last time I saw my home, in October 1945. And for a long time after the war I tried to forget. But I want to tell you.

My family had a farm outside the village of Kulykiv, Kulikov in Russian, near L'viv. That is Soviet Ukraine now, but it was part of Poland then. We were Polish citizens before the war. There were eight of us. My father, Ivan; my mother, Marta; my sisters Anna and Yasya; and my brothers Ivan and Borys and Artem. My sister Anna was a nurse in UPA, Ukrainian underground. Her husband, Aleksey, was an officer in one of the UPA forest squads farther west, near Yavoriv.

I am telling you about Anna so you will understand what happened when the Russians came in 1944. I was in Auschwitz then. I didn't learn until later. After Auschwitz I was in one of the displaced persons camps in Germany until I think September or October 1945. I went back home to Kulykiv in October, and at a Red Cross station in L'viv they told me everything that happened.

Russian NKVD killed my family. They knew about Anna, that she was a nurse for the underground or maybe that she was married to a UPA officer. Aleksey was already dead then. NKVD killed him in July 1944. They killed Anna and the rest of my family in June 1945, a month after the German war was over. Red Cross told me they shot them. Maybe they did. I want to think they did. Shooting is quick. But do you remember what you said about your mother, after the car crash, how maybe they tell you it was quick to make it easier? Sometimes I think it's like that. I went to the farm. NKVD burned it all. They burned *the house. I found some things in the ruins of the house. I found my parents' wedding rings and Anna's wedding ring. And I tell myself they were already dead. NKVD shot them and put their bodies in the house and burned the house. They were already dead when the house burned. But sometimes in the night I don't think they were.*

I wish I didn't go back home. I wish I didn't know. I wish I could think maybe they lived, it's only that we never found each other after the war. There were too many camps and lists, and we never found each other. But then I think maybe it would be harder that way, only to hope, not to know the truth.

This is the truth about me. I lied to you so many times it's okay if you don't believe me now. But I want to tell you. And maybe someday I can tell you why I lied.

The money is yours. For the trouble.

Максим Іванович Костишин
Maksym Ivanovych Kostyshyn

I SAT ON MY BED with his ten thousand State Department dollars, reading that letter. I read it over and over and over, turning the pages with numb fingers. I read it until the lines started blurring together, not making sense.

There was no brother-in-law in Toronto.

There had been a brother-in-law, but his name was Aleksey, and he died in July 1944. There was no Kyrylo Romaniuk. Whomever I had been talking to in Toronto, he wasn't Maksym's brother-in-law.

Agent Jones knew about that leaflet in Maksym's coat

pocket. He knew that Maksym would try going to the UCRF for help. He had gone to Toronto to set a trap.

It didn't make any difference now, but at least I knew. If Maksym weren't dead on the side of the road in Rome, New York, he would have been dead when he got to Toronto anyway.

Dad knocked softly on the door with a knuckle, and I jumped. I hadn't heard his footsteps on the carpet. He stuck his head in. He had his cap on; we needed to go. I had been in the bedroom for a long time.

"Shel—" he said, and I slipped the pages of Maksym's letter under a fold of the coverlet. But he caught sight of the money.

I couldn't have come up with a convincing lie if I tried. Even from the doorway, you could see they were hundred-dollar bills.

He came over slowly. He reached for the nearest bundle and held it in his hand like doubting Thomas. There was no way he didn't know whose it was and where it had come from— but still he held the bundle in his hands and thumbed through the bills without looking and said, "Where did you get it?" as though he couldn't quite make himself believe it.

"He left it for me," I said.

Dad sat down stiffly beside me on the edge of the bed and thumbed through the bills again. This time, he was counting them. He counted through each bundle one after the other, exactly as I had done.

"It's his State Department reward money," I said, "because he gave them a MiG." It hadn't occurred to me until this moment that they had only given him the reward money because they knew they would get it back, and something twisted inside me.

"Is this it? Ten thousand?"

"Ten big ones."

"What?"

"It's all he had with him. He left the rest on base. It was fifty thousand, but he had to leave forty thousand."

"Okay—listen to me, Shel. Listen to me." Dad laid the money down. He took off his cap, rested his elbows on his knees, and leaned forward a little, steepling his hands together over his face, rubbing the bridge of his nose with his fingertips. "This wasn't here, okay? We're going to get rid of it, and that's it. Nobody's going to know it was here. That's it."

"He left it for me." There would be other relatives—aunts, uncles, cousins. There had to be. Maybe some of them had survived the war; maybe some of them had managed to escape Poland before the Iron Curtain fell. There had to be some way I could get the money to them. I had to try.

"Shel." Dad lifted his head. "I've got to go in front of a House subcommittee tomorrow morning. I've got to tell them everything I know about how this happened. I can't tell them this was here, do you understand? I can't tell them he was here."

"Agent Jones knows he was here," I said.

He looked away. "I'll deal with Jones."

"He knows about the money. He'll know where it is. If they didn't find it on Maksym, he'll know where it is."

"I said I'll deal with him."

"Just tell them the truth."

"For God's sake, Shel," he said, "I'm trying to protect you."

"Tell them to do the blood work. We can prove he was innocent. We can prove that the KGB was trying to kill him."

"Blood work isn't going to prove anything." His face was in his hands again. "You know that. Even if they found ethylene glycol. How are you going to prove he didn't ingest it himself? He needed you to trust him. He would have told you anything, he would have done anything—"

"I never told you what it was," I said.

"What?"

"The poison," I said. "I never told you what it was."

NINETEEN

I STUMBLED BACK THROUGH OUR phone-room conversation in my head. I was absolutely certain that I hadn't once said "ethylene glycol" to him, or even "antifreeze," because I hadn't ever gotten that far. He had stopped listening when I said "poison."

Dad lifted his face from his hands. He looked up at me. "Shel," he started.

"I never told you. How did you know what it was?"

"Shel, listen to me," he said—

Somebody knocked on the front door.

I let him go answer it. I couldn't do it. I knew it was Jo. Who else would it be? We didn't know anybody else in Rome. The police didn't have any more reason to be knocking on our door. It was Jo, wanting to take me out for dinner or to the movies or to the dance hall or whatever else normal girlfriends did on a normal Friday night in Rome, New York; it was Jo with the evening paper in her hands—*Look, they finally got that commie.* I couldn't stand having to open the door and face her.

But it wasn't Jo.

"Good afternoon, Miss Blaine," Agent Jones said from my bedroom doorway.

He was alone. Dad hadn't come back with him. He stood in my doorway with his hat in his hand. He had his suit coat on this time, very proper. He didn't seem to notice Maksym's money still laid out plain to see atop my coverlet. That was an act, of course. There was no way he didn't notice. He was like Dad; he noticed everything.

"I'll need you to come with me, Miss Blaine," he said.

I dared to say, "Where?"

He was already turning to go back up the hallway.

"Protective custody," he said over his shoulder.

"What?"

"Colonel Blaine requested that we take you into protective custody."

"*He* requested?"

"And I'll need to debrief you," Agent Jones said, "given your proximity to the case." As if it were an afterthought, he added, "Bring the money, would you, please, Miss Blaine— and that letter."

DAD WAS GONE. HE HAD taken our car, the rental car. He was already gone by the time Agent Jones walked me out of the house—without saying goodbye, without saying a word. He had never actually said he was taking me with him to Washington. I had just assumed. He had told me to pack an overnight bag, and he had talked to somebody on a telephone, and I had been stupid enough to assume.

Agent Jones put my bag in the trunk of the falcon-gray Pontiac and opened the passenger door. He stood there waiting for me to get in, one hand resting lightly on the doorframe.

I had no idea what I was supposed to say to him. I should have been angry; I wanted to be angry. But I was just numb. I thought I was starting to get the hang of this game we were playing—and now it turned out that I had been playing the wrong game the whole time, and Agent Jones had just let me go on because he knew that meant he would win.

But when I had gotten in, and he had shut my door and gone around to the driver's side and dropped into the seat beside me, I caught a glimpse of the pistol holstered on a strap under his left arm, hidden inside the breast of his coat; that was why he was wearing the coat finally.

It was like being kicked in the gut, seeing that pistol. Something snapped off sharp and brittle inside me.

"He trusted you," I said, sitting with my hands clenched tight in my lap, helpless and aching. It was the most damning thing I could think of to say to him. "He trusted you."

I wasn't going to say a word about me—that I had trusted him too. It wasn't anything personal with me; I was clear-headed enough to recognize that. I didn't mean a thing to him. All in a day's work, all just part of the mission.

But it had been personal with Maksym. The betrayal was personal. Agent Jones had been the one listening to Maksym cry in the nights; Agent Jones had been the one there to comfort him. And Maksym had trusted him wholeheartedly, unthink-ingly. Every word out of his mouth, this whole time, had been some variation on "Jones says——" or "Jones told me——" or "Jones does this," and I didn't think he ever even realized. I didn't think he had ever made a conscious choice to trust Agent Jones, the way he had made the choice to trust me. He had trusted him implicitly, the way you're meant to trust God.

Agent Jones was occupied at the wheel for a moment, turning the engine over and releasing the hand brake and moving the gear lever into reverse. Then he said, as if he hadn't even heard, "Would you mind rolling that window up, Miss Blaine?"

"I'm sorry?" It came out polite by habit.

"Roll your window up. I'll turn the air-conditioning on."

I slapped him.

I didn't think about it first—would that make a difference to the criminal charges? But it wasn't exactly an accident. It wasn't self-defense. And I had known what to do, which would make them think I had put some thought into it. I had known to open my hand and go for the side of his face rather than his mouth; I hadn't tried to hit him with a closed fist. Somehow, I remembered what Uncle Fred told me once—that unless you knew what you were doing with a closed fist, you usually ended up hurting yourself as much as your target.

It still hurt plenty. I snatched my hand back with a gasp, fingers smarting, and reached across to fumble at the door latch with my good hand.

Agent Jones said, "Wait, Miss Blaine."

I popped the door, swinging my legs over the edge of the seat. He hadn't made a move except to put a foot on the brake. Now he threw the gear lever into neutral and put the hand brake back on.

"Your father lied to you," he said. "On my orders—to protect Kostyshyn."

I froze with the door half open, my hand on the latch, one foot on the hot pavement.

"I wanted the KGB off his trail." He spoke in that same impassive monotone; you wouldn't believe I had just slapped him across the face. "I rendered my report to the agency two hours ago. I said he was dead. I said he attempted to escape my custody, and I had no choice but to use deadly force; Agent Mancuso wasn't with me at the time. As far as Washington or anybody else is concerned, his case is closed."

He looked at me. His cheek was ribboned with the marks of my fingers, deep scarlet on the tanned skin. "I didn't kill him, Miss Blaine."

"Where is he?" It came out half a whisper, half a growl. My throat was thick with a pent-up sob.

"Where he would have been thirty hours ago," Agent Jones said, "if he hadn't decided to jump out a window."

HE WAS ASLEEP IN THE bed in Cabin 72 at the Paul Revere Motor Hotel.

I knew he was just asleep. I could see the rise and fall of his chest under the quilt; I could hear the long, steady rhythm of his breathing. But I still slipped my fingers between his fingers so I could feel the flutter of his pulse and the reassuring warmth of his hand against mine.

"Codeine and acetaminophen," said the pretty, dark-haired girl sitting in the desk chair, which she had pulled over to the bedside. Agent Jones had gone to pay for another room. "I was tired of him trying to be a hero about that ankle."

She was smartly dressed, in a slim, fitted suit of summery ash-gray linen and tall patent leather pumps, cool pearls at her ears and throat, but her hand—when she stood up to take mine—was red and callused like a farm wife's. She was barely taller than I even in those heels, which made it difficult to tell how old she was, but I thought she was probably twenty-eight or thirty. Her eyes were Maksym's same shade of warm honey brown. The dimple at the corner of her smile was the same.

"I'm Anna," she said. "You must be Miss Blaine."

I shook her hand numbly.

"Shelby," I managed. Stupidly, all I could think just then was, *I've had my tongue in your little brother's mouth*—and I had the uncomfortable feeling that she could tell just by looking at me. Her gaze was very keen.

But she just smiled at me. Her grip was strong, but it was friendly.

"Shelby," she repeated carefully—exactly as Maksym had done the first time we met. "Maks told me about you. He told me how much you've done for him."

And I, fumbling a little, still mortified by the thought of that kiss, said, "He told me you were dead."

I didn't mean it spitefully. I meant only that I didn't understand—that she was supposed to be dead in June 1945 in some place called Kulykiv, Kulikov in Russian, and yet here she was alive and well in July 1955 in Rome, New York; that evidently that letter had been just one more lie in Maksym's long string of lies stretching all the way back to Bornholm; that I had no idea who was telling me the truth anymore—but she must have taken it as a sort of accusation. Her smile slipped away, her face shuttering.

She dropped my hand.

"We tried to find him," she said. "We tried so hard. Aleks traced him to the labor office in Heidelberg. He traced him that far, through friends in the Polish resistance. But we couldn't find him."

"He ran away," I said. "I don't think he was in Heidelberg very long."

Anna nodded, mouth tight. She looked suddenly older and harder. In that moment, I could see the fine strands of gray shot through her glossy dark hair; I could see the sharp lines of grief and exhaustion at the corners of her laughing eyes. She knew where Maksym had been after Heidelberg.

"And of course after the war we wrote to all the displaced persons camps. We wrote to all the agencies, all the volunteer organizations—the Red Cross, the UNRRA, the Polish relief funds, the Ukrainian relief funds." She sat gingerly on the end of the bed and indicated for me to take the desk chair. "But they were already starting to make lists—the NKVD, the secret police. They were making lists of people who had fought in the underground, deporting them to the labor camps. We were afraid they had our names on a list. We decided to leave Kulykiv. And Kyrylo thought—my husband, my second husband . . ." She looked up, making an attempt at a smile. Her face was drawn. "You talked to him earlier, I think. He said you rang."

"Yes." I fitted this piece into the puzzle in my head. Maksym couldn't know that Kyrylo Romaniuk was his brother-in-law because in October 1943 he wasn't yet.

"Kyrylo thought it would be safer if they believed we were already dead—safer for us to try to leave the occupation zone. So we burned the farm. We made it look as if the NKVD had done it. We made it look as if we had died there. We left the Soviet zone under false names, false documents. We left." Anna smoothed her skirt absently, then twisted her hands together tightly on her lap. "We thought—both of us, Kyrylo and I—we thought we could keep looking for Maks in the West. I had some Red Cross contacts, and he had a friend with good connections in British intelligence. We thought it would be easier, actually—to go to the camps in person, to talk to people who might have seen him, who might be able to tell us—"

She cut herself off. Her eyes were rimmed red.

"There are no excuses," she said. "I keep making excuses. We left him. We left him."

"You didn't know—" I started.

"That he would try to go back home?" Her voice was sharp. "You didn't even know he was still alive."

"We should have stayed until we knew."

"It isn't your fault," I said softly. "Anna, that isn't what I meant."

"We should have stayed," she said.

"It isn't your fault. I'm sure he doesn't think so. I'm sure all he cares about is that you're alive—that he gets to see you again."

I expected her to snap at me. I would have snapped at me. What did I know? I had known her brother for not quite three days. How could I have any idea what had gone through his head when he learned, ten years on, that his family was alive and safe in the West while he had been left behind?

But she didn't snap at me. She gave me another small smile, wan but sincere.

"He likes you very much," she said.

"Well, I gave him a lot of whiskey," I said.

I was making a joke, a stupid joke, but her face went tight again.

"Yes," she said grimly. "That idiot nearly killed him. I wonder if it ever occurred to him that you don't actually need to use the poison to fake a poisoning."

"What idiot?"

Her lips pursed. "I didn't mean idiot," she said. "He isn't an idiot. I'm sorry. But it was a stupid plan."

"What idiot?"

"Agent Jones," she said.

TWENTY

AGENT JONES WAS SITTING WITH a neat Scotch, a cigarette, and a newspaper at a table in the bar.

It took me a moment to spot him. It was a little past six o'clock, still broad daylight, but the barroom was windowless and lit only dimly with oil lamps—for the colonial atmosphere, I supposed, though the effect was spoiled somewhat by the pianist coaxing "Love Is Here to Stay" out of the baby grand in the corner. And there was a bit of a crowd, everybody starting to descend on the bar for pre-dinner drinks on a Friday night. Agent Jones was garnering some annoyed looks—he was sitting alone at a table for two—but nobody was actually daring to take it up with him. He did look rather like a mafioso sitting there with his stony face and his expensive dark suit. I wondered whether he still had that pistol under his coat.

I started working my way over to him through wafting clouds of cigarette smoke and cocktail chatter. A red-jacketed waiter materialized beside me.

"Identification, miss?"

"I'm sorry?"

"You need to be eighteen to be in the bar."

"I am eighteen."

"Do you have identification, a driver's license?"

"She's with me," Agent Jones said without looking up from his paper.

I had no idea how he did it. He didn't even raise his voice, didn't even look my way, and yet suddenly people were melting aside, clearing a path for me, and the waiter was waving me along to the table with a smile.

"Good evening, Miss Blaine," Agent Jones said, still studying his paper.

I took my seat across the table—*my* seat, the seat he had meant for me. He knew I would come. He had been sitting here waiting for me.

It was infuriating to be so manageable.

The table was low and intimate, clearly meant for a couple. I had to curve my legs out awkwardly to the side to keep from accidentally bumping into him under the kitschy red-and-white checkered tablecloth. His newspaper took up the entire tabletop.

As if he had only just realized this, he folded the paper up and placed his whiskey glass neatly atop it, making a show of granting me a grudging favor.

I caught a glimpse of the masthead in the flickering lamplight before his glass obscured it: *Die Zeit*. It was a Hamburg paper. I recognized it from the bus station newsstand in Kaiserslautern.

"Why are you reading a German paper?" I asked.

"Did you ever read American papers in Germany?" he asked, taking out his cigarette.

"Well—yes. But that's different. That's how we got news from home."

He put on his act of pretending not to hear. "Do you want a drink, Miss Blaine?"

I looked at him, his tanned face all shadows and sharp angles in the lamplight, his dark blond hair in its government-issue crew cut, his expressionless blue-green eyes, and my stomach started folding slowly over on itself.

"*Du bist Deutscher?*" I asked.

He pulled one last quick drag on his cigarette, then stubbed it out in the ashtray, exhaling a soft, smoky breath.

"Well done," he said.

I wasn't sure whether he was complimenting my pronunciation or congratulating me for figuring him out. "Are you from Hamburg?"

"Dresden," he said.

It was like saying a dirty word in polite company, saying *Dresden*. You flinched and said something else as quickly as you could, trying to fill the uncomfortable silence. Dad had flown in the firebombing raids. I knew because they were listed in the operational histories in his old squadron scrapbooks. He had never said a word about them. He would talk about some of the other missions he had flown. He wouldn't talk about Dresden.

And Dresden was in East Germany, the Soviet zone.

My stomach folded over again, slippery with unease. Sweat sprang out lightly on my palms. I dropped my hands to my lap. Could you want vengeance so badly? Could you want it so badly that you would join one old enemy to fight another?

"Yes," I said. "Yes, I want a drink."

"Champagne for the lady," Agent Jones said to a passing red jacket.

He had taken care that we were in a public place. We were safely visible, but we wouldn't be overheard. He wanted to talk. He only wanted to talk.

"You're KGB," I said.

"Out of curiosity, Miss Blaine," he said, tipping back a swallow of whiskey, "what made you so sure Kostyshyn wasn't?"

"Before I knew you poisoned him, you mean?"

"Yesterday afternoon. You had two opportunities to turn him in—to the police and to your father. You had already decided to help him."

"If you were on the run," I said, folding my hands together tightly in my lap, "if I found you hiding in my linen closet, and we were alone in the house, and you had a gun—you wouldn't stand there in my kitchen trying to explain yourself to me."

"Probably not, unless I also had a debilitating injury, a pronounced foreign accent, no knowledge of the local geography, and no cash on hand smaller than hundreds. Then I might take my chances with you."

My face flushed. "It's a moot point. He isn't KGB."

"And I didn't poison him. Technically."

"You told Anna you did."

"Yes."

"She thinks it was all some elaborate plan to get him off base. But it wasn't, was it? You were trying to kill him. And then you tried to cover your tracks by giving me the antidote."

"Did your father tell you how he knew?"

"What?"

"He said you caught him out. Did he tell you how he knew the poison?"

184

The red jacket set a champagne coupe before me, and I unfolded my sweating hands to wrap my fingers around the cool glass stem. "No."

Agent Jones reached inside the breast of his coat, took out a wallet photograph, and laid it on the table in front of me. "Do you recognize him?"

The man in the photograph was in Air Force dress uniform. It was an official portrait, the sort that would hang framed on the wall in squadron headquarters, with the Stars and Stripes draped dramatically in the background. I did recognize him. He had been in Dad's air intelligence squadron at Ramstein. He and his wife had come to some of Mom's house parties; I remembered the place cards. *Captain and Mrs. Charles Fletcher.* Their daughter Carrie had been a few years behind me at Rhine High.

"I don't think so," I said. I couldn't tell where he was going, and I wasn't going to give him anything without making him work for it.

Agent Jones's face was blank, but I knew he knew I was lying. But he played along.

"Captain Charles Fletcher," he said. "He's with intelligence at Ramstein. Your father's old squadron."

"I wouldn't know."

"They didn't work closely together. Their specialties don't overlap. Your father's in technical intelligence, Fletcher's in cryptanalytics—code breaking. And evidently they weren't family friends." His voice was dry. "But your father met Fletcher privately off base in Landstuhl last month."

"How do you know?"

Agent Jones returned the photograph to his coat pocket.

"I was there," he said, "observing the meeting. I've been watching Fletcher for a year and a half."

I remembered suddenly that he had been a field agent until three weeks ago. "Why?"

"Fletcher is a Soviet agent," he said.

"A friend of yours?" I asked cuttingly.

Agent Jones slipped his cigarette pack from his breast pocket, picked out another cigarette reflectively, tapped it twice against the top of the pack, and dipped his head to light it with his Zippo.

"My father," he said around his cigarette, "is what the Nazis considered *Deutschblütiger*, pure German blood. My mother is Jewish. Their marriage would have been illegal under the Nuremberg Laws. We left Germany in the spring of 1936, when I was eleven. My father changed our name to the most American name he could think of because he was ashamed to have a German name." He put his lighter back in his pocket. "I was naturalized as an American citizen when I deployed with the Ninetieth. I've been an American longer than I was a German. I'm not on some East German vendetta. You don't have to trust me, Miss Blaine, but maybe you can hear me out before you make up your mind."

"I'm sorry," I said quietly.

"Kostyshyn's defection was a headache for Moscow. Not only was he an officer with enough rank to have access to some sensitive intelligence, he was one of two pilots at Baltiysk— the base in Kaliningrad—chosen to test-fly their newest MiG prototype. They needed to control the damage. They needed to know what he was telling us. Ideally, they could discredit him by throwing doubt on whether his defection was genuine—make us question whether any intelligence we got from him was actually usable. But they needed one of their people in on the debriefing process."

I looked intently into my champagne coupe, watching the little bubbles stream up to the surface and dance apart. I still couldn't tell where he was going, but I was starting to be afraid of wherever it was.

"Thanks to their agent Fletcher, Moscow knew your father had been gathering intelligence on this new MiG for over a year. They knew your father would be the one called in to debrief Kostyshyn for Air Force intelligence. The meeting with Fletcher in Landstuhl was their attempt to recruit him. They couldn't risk his refusal; they'd have shown their hand. So they made sure they could coerce his cooperation."

I looked into my champagne coupe and said, "Coerce how?"

"The meeting in Landstuhl was on June seventh," Agent Jones said.

June seventh—the day after Mom died.

I didn't remember Dad going to Landstuhl that day. Everything after the crash was a blur in my head. But I wouldn't have questioned his being gone. He still had things to do; I knew that. The world hadn't stopped turning because my mother was dead.

"Did they kill her?" I asked. My throat was tight.

"Maybe. There isn't any way to prove it. There weren't any witnesses."

"But it could have been a hit-and-run."

"It could have been."

I sipped a mouthful of champagne and held it behind my teeth for a moment, feeling it light and cool on my aching tongue. The implications would have been obvious to Dad. If the KGB could kill Mom in her car on the autobahn, they could kill him. Or they could kill me. He would have seen no option but to cooperate.

Agent Jones said, "The problem from the agency's perspective was that at that point we didn't know who initiated the Landstuhl meeting. Fletcher communicated to his KGB case officer that the meeting was a go. We didn't know who initiated it. There was a possibility that your father was the one who sought Fletcher out. There was a possibility that your mother's accident was just an accident and that your father indicated an interest in recruitment as a result. It happens sometimes in the wake of tragedy. There's no ideological motivation, just disillusionment. Maybe just the need to make a clean break from an old life."

I swallowed my champagne carefully. "You thought he was working for the KGB by choice."

"I kept asking myself the question—if it wasn't by choice, why not come to us? Why not alert the agency? He had the ability; he had agency contacts. We could have taken both of you into protective custody. There wasn't any reason for him to keep quiet unless he was acting by choice." Agent Jones pulled at his cigarette. "Or unless he believed the agency had been compromised."

"He didn't trust you," I said. "He thought you were a Red

agent. Wednesday night—he told me he thought you were a Red agent."

"Because he knew he wasn't the only KGB operative assigned to Kostyshyn's case. He knew that for a fact. He'd been given coordinates for a dead drop here in Rome . . ." He paused, glancing up; he must have caught the look on my face. "A dead drop. No live contact with the other operative. You both have the coordinates, that's it. You make the drop; they come along later and pick it up. You never actually meet."

"Oh."

"So he knew there was at least one other KGB agent on the case. Didn't know who it was. He had the coordinates and instructions for making the drops, no other method of contact. Could be anybody. Somebody at Griffiss, somebody in Rome, somebody on Kimball's FBI team from Utica—"

"Or you."

"Or me. He couldn't risk trusting the wrong person." Agent Jones held his cigarette in two fingers and turned his glass in slow circles under his fingertips, swirling the whiskey. "But yesterday morning I caught him pouring antifreeze into Kostyshyn's drink. He didn't have much choice but to start talking to me."

"I don't understand."

"He explained himself. He showed me the coordinates for the drop. He admitted that he had agreed to expose Kostyshyn as a KGB plant and hand him back over to Moscow. He couldn't abort his mission; this other operative almost certainly has orders to eliminate him if he tries. But he thought he could get Kostyshyn out." He brushed the tip of his cigarette carefully against the rim of the ashtray. "The symptoms of ethylene glycol poisoning look like a lot of other things. His KGB controllers wouldn't jump to conclude that Kostyshyn had been poisoned. Even if they got to poison, they wouldn't jump to conclude he had done it. So—forty milliliters of antifreeze in a bottle of Coca-Cola during a coffee break. He was counting on Kostyshyn being moved to the base hospital once symptoms presented. He was going to fake a death record and try to get him off base from there; the hospital's just inside the south gate. He was taking a calculated risk."

I thought of Uncle Fred that day in the barn in Ohio—of the dare that had almost killed him. I had never asked him who had dared him. It had never occurred to me to ask, maybe because I had always half known. Of course it had been his brother.

"And you let him?"

"He was right. The only way to get the KGB off Kostyshyn's trail was to make them think he was dead." Agent Jones shrugged a little. "And then Kostyshyn jumped out a window. He thought he was being taken back to Washington. His symptoms hadn't presented yet. He didn't know he'd been poisoned."

"That's what I mean," I said. "I don't understand. Anna's right. You didn't even need to poison him. You could have at least told him you were going to give him the antidote. You could have told him you were trying to help him."

Agent Jones put his cigarette back in his mouth. His face was expressionless.

"Your father never had the chance," he said. "He and Kostyshyn were never alone."

"But you could have told him."

He didn't say anything—just sat there pulling at his cigarette as though he were waiting for me to pass the test.

"Because you thought it was him," I realized. "Because you thought Maksym was the other KGB agent."

"Because I made a mistake," Agent Jones said.

TWENTY-ONE

NOISE INTRUDED BETWEEN US FOR a moment—snatches of conversation, the ripple of piano keys, the clink of glassware. I had almost forgotten we were in the middle of an ordinary motel bar on an ordinary Friday night in Rome, New York.

Agent Jones exhaled softly. I couldn't tell whether it was a laugh or a sigh. Either way, it was unexpected. It made him seem human and vulnerable. It was as if he had slipped off a mask just for a second, and you knew he was actually capable of laughing and sighing and making mistakes.

"Kostyshyn lied to your father," he said. "He lied to me when I debriefed him, and he lied to your father. He told your father the same story he told me: His wingman, Andreyev, shot him down on orders from Baltiysk just before he crossed into Danish airspace. I didn't have photographs of the plane when I debriefed him in Washington last month. Kostyshyn didn't realize that your father did. DSIS just released them to us—Danish intelligence. The plane wasn't shot down. There wasn't any external weapons damage. The only weapons damage was to the interior of the cockpit. Kostyshyn set an explosive before he ejected. Maybe a timed bomb, maybe not. Could have been a hand grenade. He'd have had time to eject after he pulled the pin."

I swallowed another mouthful of champagne. Maksym had told me it was an electrical malfunction—but then he had also told me he was Russian, from Leningrad. At that point, he was saying anything and everything he could think of to stop me from going up to base without coming right out and saying *why*.

He had figured out who had poisoned him.

He must have known as soon as I told him that the poisoning had most likely happened Thursday morning. He must have remembered exactly what he drank and who had given it to him.

He must have known that Dad was on KGB orders.

Why hadn't he told me? Why on earth had he spun that whole story about Leningrad instead of just giving me the truth?

"I thought it was a setup," Agent Jones said. "The KGB was planning to run your father as an agent inside Griffiss; Kostyshyn's defection was set up to test his reliability. On the off chance that the defection was genuine, I was prepared to help him. But I wasn't going to reveal anything to him until I knew. I wasn't going to risk it."

"But you made a mistake."

"I made a mistake. I know why he lied." Agent Jones flicked ash from his cigarette. "I went back," he said. "Yesterday afternoon, I went back and looked at everything we had from DSIS. Made some calls and got everything I could get from British intelligence; they had Kostyshyn for three days in June. Two points of interest from the Brits. One—" He glanced up. "The KGB executed Zhenya Andreyev sometime in mid-June."

My heart tightened into a fist. "Because he didn't shoot Maksym down."

"I don't know how much of it they planned beforehand—Kostyshyn and Andreyev. I don't know if Kostyshyn told Andreyev he was planning to defect. It would have been risky. Andreyev had excellent party credentials. His father had been a member of the Politburo. But in any case, Andreyev disobeyed the shootdown order. He made a show of shooting at Kostyshyn, and Kostyshyn made a show of being shot at. The grenade—the bomb, whatever it was—was for the benefit of Andreyev's cockpit camera. Kostyshyn must have been hoping that the detonation would look like an autocannon hit on film." Agent Jones rolled his cigarette absently between his fingertips. "Kostyshyn lied to protect Andreyev. He didn't anticipate that the Danes would be able to salvage his MiG. Those photographs were Andreyev's death warrant. Somebody in DSIS leaked them to Moscow."

"Does he know?" I asked, clenching the stem of my champagne coupe. "Maksym. Does he know Andreyev is dead?"

"No."

"Are you going to tell him?"

"No," Agent Jones said.

"He needs to know." My throat was tight. I was thinking of that letter. *It would be harder that way—only to hope, not to know the truth.* "I think he would want to know."

"Given the choice," Agent Jones said, "between believing you kept a friend alive and knowing you killed him—"

"The KGB killed him."

"You know that objectively. It doesn't make a difference in the middle of the night."

"He trusts you," I said. "He trusts you more than he trusts anyone else. What if he finds out that you knew the truth and didn't tell him? He needs to know. He needs to hear it from you."

"I wasn't his first handler." The mask had gone back up; Agent Jones's face was stone blank. "He'd already been through a week and a half of debriefing before I was assigned to him—ten straight days. CIA, FBI, Department of Defense. Three days with MI6 in London before that; they cut a deal with us behind Copenhagen's back. Twelve-hour sessions in English. He didn't have any problem with English; he picked it up in UN camps after the war. But his handler told him he wasn't allowed to use Russian even outside the debriefing room, even in private. No access to any materials in Russian—no newspapers, no books, no music. And he stopped talking. The handler thought he was being belligerent. The truth is he was homesick. He was acutely depressed, he was lonely, he was ashamed of what he'd done, and he was homesick. It didn't have anything to do with ideology. He isn't a communist; he joined the party three years ago so they would let him into flight school. He isn't Russian. But that's what he knows. That's the world he understands. He left behind everything and everyone familiar, and he can never go back." Agent Jones was grinding the tip of his cigarette slowly and deliberately to ash against the rim of the tray. "One of his FBI interrogators recognized what was going on. If he hadn't, I doubt Kostyshyn would have lasted to the end of that week. To be honest, Miss Blaine," he said, "when I saw that window open yesterday morning, I didn't assume he was trying to run. I'm not going to tell him his best friend is dead for helping him defect." He hesitated. "And he trusts *you*. That's why you're here."

I looked into my champagne coupe, swallowing thickly. I didn't know what to say to that. He was right: It would shatter Maksym to know he had lost Zhenya Andreyev—to know that despite his best efforts his defection had cost Zhenya's life. But sooner or later he would find out. Sooner or later, he would find out that Agent Jones had kept him deliberately in the dark—and then he would have lost both of them. Wasn't that worse?

"You said there was something else from British intelligence," I said tightly.

"There had been a question from the beginning about Kostyshyn's family—about their involvement with the Ukrainian underground during the war. MiG pilots are supposed to be politically unimpeachable. That doesn't make it impossible: Two years ago, we took in a MiG-15 pilot whose father was a Polish army officer killed by the Soviets in 1939. But according to British intelligence, Kostyshyn's internal file was absolutely clean. It shouldn't have been. If his family had been executed by the NKVD, his file should have been marked." Agent Jones dropped his cigarette stub into the pile of feathery gray ashes. "You could take that one of two ways. Either he told us they had been executed to give his cover story plausibility, to give himself a reason to defect—or he told us they had been executed because he believed they had been executed. I asked MI6 to look into their immigration records."

"And they found Anna."

"They found all of them. Ivan and Marta Kostyshyn settled in England after the war. Anna and her second husband, Kyrylo Romaniuk, emigrated from England to Ontario in '47. He's a partner in his uncle's law firm in Toronto. She's an emergency room pediatrician at the children's hospital." Agent Jones held his whiskey glass in his fingers and said, "Most cases of ethylene glycol poisoning occur in children. Accidental ingestion. She's dealt with it before."

He had taken out the motel room—Cabin 72, closest to the woods and least visible from the highway and the main building—and gone to Toronto to get Anna. *Mrs. Kobryn.* That must have been her first husband's name—Aleksey Kobryn.

"I needed an excuse," Agent Jones said. "I needed a reason to go up to Toronto, and I needed to keep Kimball and the FBI busy while I did."

"You planted those addresses in Maksym's bags," I guessed.

"Last night. Kimball's people and the police had already been over the room. Showed them up a bit when I found the cache. CIA efficiency," he said dryly. "A little too efficient. The agency sent Mancuso up from the city this morning. They thought Kostyshyn and I were working together. So I had him breathing down my neck when you let slip that you knew where Kostyshyn was. All I could do was give you the key and the antidote and let you put it together. I was already committed to Toronto. Had to set Mancuso on a wild-goose chase looking through admission records at the hospital so I could get a word alone with Anna."

"I couldn't figure out what the room was for," I admitted.

He shrugged. "It was a toss-up. It would have been risky trying to get him here. But the quicker we could get him out of your house, the better. If they realized he was with you . . ."

He didn't finish. I didn't have to ask whom he meant by *they*.

"Do you have any idea who it is? The other agent?"

"Not yet. We're watching the dead drop." He tipped back

his whiskey. "I happened to 'find' the coordinates on Kostyshyn when we took him into custody. That's where Mancuso is. I sent him up to the lake to take a look. Got him out of the way while I brought Kostyshyn here."

"The lake?"

"Delta Lake."

"The coordinates were for Delta Lake?"

He was looking at me now. "Is something wrong, Miss Blaine?"

"No—nothing. It's just—"

I was just thinking of Jo Matheson—bored, beautiful Jo Matheson with her engineering degree and nothing to do but host Friday afternoon bridge club—who went up to paint at the lake all the time because you pretty much had the place to yourself, even in the summer; who had just happened to be here at the motel in the same exact twenty-minute window of time as I this morning; who had somehow managed to play an entire round of golf in ninety-degree heat without mussing her makeup or chipping her perfectly manicured nails.

My hands were sweating again.

"I think," I said carefully, "I think I might know who it is. I think she knows we brought Maksym here."

A red jacket stepped up politely to the table.

"Good evening, Miss Kobryn, Mr. Kobryn," he said, smiling at us. "Sir, Mrs. Kobryn is trying to reach you on the telephone."

TWENTY-TWO

ANNA MET US AT THE cabin door, tight-lipped but calm.

"She said she was from the front desk," she told Agent Jones. "She said she had a message."

Jo Matheson lay on the bare floor beside the woodstove. She was wearing the sunflower-yellow rayon uniform of the motel's lobby staff. Her suit jacket was open; bloodstained bath towels swathed her waist. I thought she was dead. She was lying there limp and white-faced and bloody, and I thought she was dead there on the cabin floor. I shrank against the timber-paneled wall behind Agent Jones, swallowing a lurch of bile.

Agent Jones holstered his pistol under his arm and went over to look at the body.

"I thought you sent her," Anna said to him quietly, shutting the door. "It was stupid of me." Her face was hard and tight. She was angry at herself.

Agent Jones threw a glance toward the bedroom doorway as he crouched beside Jo.

"He's fine," Anna said. "Still asleep."

"Anybody hear the shot?"

"No, I don't think so. Maks had a silencer on the pistol. The other cabins are empty—except for seventy-four, but they're at dinner."

Agent Jones leaned over to look at the wound. They were both being brisk and cold and professional, and I had the sudden feeling of being a little kid watching the adults at work.

"Is she stable? I'd rather not have to explain this in the emergency room at Murphy Memorial."

"For now, yes."

My shoulders loosened just a little against the panels. *Stable.* Alive. Wounded and unconscious, not dead.

"Can she travel? I'll get Mancuso to take her down to the city."

Anna hesitated. "You mean take Agent Mancuso into confidence."

"We're going to have to. Everything's going to come out when she starts talking. Unless you want to go ahead and deal with that here." Agent Jones's voice was perfectly level, frighteningly level; I couldn't tell whether he was being serious.

"And Maks, when they find out he's alive? What happens to him? He goes back to the Air Force? He goes back to the CIA for more debriefing?"

Agent Jones said something to her in a low voice. I couldn't tell what he said; it must have been something in Russian—or Ukrainian, I supposed. Whatever it was, Anna nodded once, apparently satisfied.

"I need gauze dressings," she said, "actual dressings. She can't travel like this."

"Make me a list of what you need. I'll get it."

"Do you think she reported it?" I asked.

They both looked up at me sharply. I was pretty sure they had forgotten I was there.

"She knew about this room," I said carefully to Agent Jones. "I think she must have seen me with you downtown this morning and followed me here. She must have been watching it. She must have seen you bring Maksym." I swallowed another knot of bile; my stomach was still churning. "Do you think she would have had a chance to report it?"

I couldn't say exactly what I meant. I couldn't say, *Do you think she had a chance to report Dad?*—not in front of Anna. I didn't think Anna knew anything about Dad and the KGB. I didn't think Agent Jones had told her anything. He had told her that he was the one who poisoned Maksym.

But he knew what I meant. Jo could have reported to her case officer that Maksym was alive and safe in CIA custody. She could have reported that I had been in a CIA officer's car this morning.

She could have reported that Dad had disobeyed his orders and aborted his mission.

Agent Jones got up.

"I'm going to make a phone call," he said to Anna. "I'll be back for that list."

I SAT IN THE BEDROOM with the door shut, camping myself in the desk chair with my legs folded up, turning slowly through the pages of the photo album Anna must have brought with her to show Maksym. Most of the photos were recent—color photos of people and places and things in Toronto, or what I assumed was Toronto. There was a man of thirty or so who must have been Kyrylo, and a dark-haired, gray-eyed boy of maybe ten who must have been Mykola, and two younger girls of indeterminate age who looked exactly like Anna despite having Kyrylo's mouse-blond hair. There were photos of Christmases and baptisms and birthdays and weddings, all carefully dated and captioned; there were big family photos flocked with dimpled, dark-haired siblings and aunts and uncles and cousins, unmistakably Kostyshyn.

There was one lone photograph on its own page at the very back of the album—a younger Anna, probably about my age, with a boy in military uniform. He hadn't been in any of the other photos; he wasn't a young Kyrylo. There was no date or caption on this photo, and it was a rather scratched and grainy old black-and-white print, but I knew even without really being able to tell eye color or hair color that he was Aleksey Kobryn, Anna's first husband, Mykola's father, who died in July 1944.

I shut the album. It felt suddenly profane to be looking through it. I pulled the novel from her handbag instead. It was some sort of medieval adventure story, *The Two Towers*—swords and horses and monsters—not at all the sort of book I would have imagined her reading. But then, I had no idea what sort of book I imagined her reading. My idea of her had been complicated by the fact that she had calmly shot a girl an hour ago.

She was with Jo in the other room. Jo was awake; at one point I heard Anna say something to her softly, and I heard her say something back. I couldn't stand being in there. I didn't have anything to say to Jo. I didn't want to listen to explanations or excuses, and I didn't trust myself to be gracious enough to listen to an apology. I didn't know how Anna could do it. I supposed she could do it because her brother was alive, not smashed against an overpass pylon.

Maksym was still asleep. I thought he had woken up once. He gave a convulsive little start, flinging an arm out across the sheets and mumbling something, but he was already asleep again when I leaned over to look. For a split second, I had the reckless urge to try kissing his cheek, the way they do in movies, but I was a quarter afraid he would wake up just as I bent over him, and I was three-quarters afraid Anna would walk in on me.

I went into the bathroom to splash cold water on my face. I was tired and headachy; I was starving. The last thing I had eaten today was that buttered roll at brunch with Jo, a lifetime ago.

Maksym was awake when I went back into the room.

He had turned over onto his side to face me; he had heard somebody behind the bathroom door. He blinked at me as though he couldn't quite make sense of me in this context.

"Hello," he said.

"Hello," I said—and then, with a little twinge of doubt, "you weren't awake this whole time, were you?"

"No. Sleeping. Anna gave me . . . something." His voice was still thick with sleep; he wasn't all the way awake yet. "Something for the ankle."

"Codeine."

"Yeah, codeine. I think."

I sat down on the edge of the bed. My tongue was tied. His world had changed so much since I had seen him last, five hours ago. Both of our worlds had changed so much. Seeing him now—it was like seeing somebody familiar and not quite being able to remember their name, and feeling flustered because you know you should remember it, but all you can do is smile and make stupid small talk while you wait for the memory to click back into place.

"How are you feeling? Do you need anything? Water or anything? Anna's in the other room; I can get her if you—"

He didn't share any compunction for small talk. He reached up, pulled me down to him, and kissed me.

"Anna's in the other room," I repeated in warning, putting my hands on his shoulders.

He lay there looking up at me, his hands on my waist, his brow furrowed into that little scowl. I could see him trying to put things together.

"Jones brought you here," he said.

"Yes."

"He told you? About Colonel Blaine? About . . ." He hesitated. He shut his eyes as though he had to concentrate to make the words come out right. "The poison. Who did it."

"He told me," I said softly. "Maksym—why on earth didn't you tell me? Why on earth did you *leave the house*?—in broad daylight, on a broken ankle, knowing the police were out there looking for you—"

He let out a little breath. "I tried to tell you. I said, 'Don't go to Colonel Blaine. Maybe we can wait for Jones.' And you said—"

"All right—but if you had said, 'Don't go to Colonel Blaine; he's the one who poisoned me'—"

"If I told you Colonel Blaine was working for KGB—if KGB thought you knew—they would kill you." He searched over my face, brow still furrowed. "I'm sorry," he said. "I'm sorry to lie. It was for you. Being careful for you."

He tried to kiss me again. I turned my head away. My throat was tight; my heart was tight.

I couldn't do it. I couldn't do it, no matter what Agent Jones said. I couldn't demand the truth from him and then lie to him in return.

"Zhenya Andreyev is dead," I said.

He went very still.

I drew an aching breath. "The KGB killed him. They knew he didn't shoot you down. They knew——"

"I know," he said.

"What?"

"I know. I mean——I thought probably. When Colonel Blaine showed me the photos, I thought probably. I didn't know there were photos. If somebody made photos, KGB have them. It would be stupid not to think so."

I held his bruised face between my hands, brushing my thumbs gently across his cheekbones. "I'm sorry. Maksym, I'm so sorry."

He exhaled softly. I could feel him tensed beneath me.

"It's good to know," he said. "Not easy, but good." He was silent for a moment; then he added, "It's good to know Colonel Blaine isn't KGB——not really KGB. For a while, I thought maybe he gave KGB the photos. I would kill him if he did that."

He didn't say it with anger or with hatred——that was what made it chilling. He said it calmly, matter-of-factly, as if it only made sense.

Then he looked up at me, and his face softened.

"I'm sorry," he said.

"We could do this all day, couldn't we? 'I'm sorry; no, *I'm* sorry; no, *I'm* sorry—'"

I was trying to make a joke, but all at once I was crying into his shoulder. I didn't know why. I couldn't have told him why if he had asked. I wasn't crying for Zhenya Andreyev, not really, and I didn't know why I should have been crying for Mom—here, in this moment, when it had been more than a month and I hadn't even cried for her at Ramstein.

But he didn't ask. He didn't say anything. He held me close against him, and I cried until I couldn't cry any more.

AGENT JONES GOT BACK WITH Anna's supplies a little before eight o'clock. Agent Mancuso was with him. There was a stretch of muffled busyness in the other room. Maksym had drifted off to sleep again, and I had gingerly extricated myself from his arms and retreated to the desk chair before I accidentally fell asleep there in the bed with him.

Somebody knocked on the bedroom door—two quick, sharp raps with a knuckle. Agent Jones came in, shutting the door behind him and leaning on it as though he were bracing to defend the keep against Orcs.

"I had an agent waiting on the ground at National when your father's flight touched down," he told me. "We've got him in a safe house now."

"An agent you trust?"

"An agent I trust."

I closed Anna's novel and sat there with it heavy on my lap, my hands folded tightly over the cover. I should have been relieved, but I didn't feel relieved. I felt sick to my stomach and on edge and angry, though I wasn't sure whom I was angry at.

"You shouldn't have let him go in the first place," I said to Agent Jones. "He should have been in protective custody too. They've probably been onto him since Jo saw me in your car this morning."

"It was his decision. He didn't want to roll up the operation just yet. If we took him in, we lost our chance at uncovering the rest of the network. We didn't have any other leads."

"But now you have Jo."

"Mrs. Matheson. Yes."

I realized I was angry at myself.

"I should have put it together sooner. I wondered why she was at the motel this morning."

Agent Jones gave me a flat little look. "That wasn't much to go on."

"I should have put it together."

"If you want another chance," he said, "I'll give you a recommendation."

"What?"

"For the agency. I'll give you a recommendation."

"You mean to join the CIA."

"You've got time to think about it. You'll need your bachelor's degree if you want anything more than secretary work." He turned to go, opening the door. "But you should think about it."

EPILOGUE

I SAW JO ONCE DURING debriefing.

I wasn't sure where they were keeping her, or whether she was technically even under arrest yet or still just a "person of interest"; she wasn't in prison clothes. At any rate, they did all our CIA debriefings at the same place—the same building, the CIA headquarters building at Navy Hill in Washington— and I saw her one morning in the debriefing room, in the interval between the end of her debriefing session and the start of mine. She was sitting there in the chair in front of the desk while two guys in suits—her interrogator and her lawyer?— argued over some paperwork point by point and consulted a third party on the telephone. I couldn't imagine it was protocol for us to be in the same room or to talk to each other, but my minder, not seeming to care, took the opportunity to sneak herself a cigarette just outside the doorway while we waited for the argument to be sorted out.

Jo gave me a bit of that arch smile, just a little hollow, and said, "Hello, Blaine."

She didn't look anything like you would expect a captured spy to look. She hadn't suddenly transformed into the dastardly caricature of a Red spy from one of our propaganda posters.

She was sitting with her long legs stretched out as though she were in a chaise lounge on a Miami beach; she looked tired, that was it. She was still managing to keep up her nails.

I thought of all the things I could say, all the things you *should* say to a caught spy, and I said the only thing I cared about saying.

"You knew they killed her," I said.

She had never asked me about Mom. She had grilled me over everything else. She had never asked one question about Mom.

She opened her mouth; then she closed it. She looked away. "Yes," she said.

And that was that. That was the only thing that mattered to me about Jo Matheson. I didn't say anything else to her, and she didn't look at me again.

The argument ended; my minder finished her smoke; they took Jo out. I didn't see her any more after that. It couldn't have been protocol for us to see each other. In retrospect, I thought they were probably trying to see whether either of us—given the chance to talk freely—would spill something useful about Maksym.

It had been five weeks since he vanished without a trace from Cabin 72 at the Paul Revere Motor Hotel in Rome, New York.

THEY ASKED ME IN DEBRIEFING, of course, more than once and in different ways—whether I had any guesses as to his whereabouts, whether I had been given any means of contacting him by Agent Jones or by Maksym himself. I gave them the same answers again and again: I'd had my own room that night at the Paul Revere; Anna and Maksym had already been gone when I woke up the next morning; no, I didn't have any guesses; no, I hadn't been given any means of contact. I knew they thought I was lying.

They gave us two days to go to Columbus when the debriefing sessions were over—two days only; we had to be back in Washington for the start of the trial on Monday. It was just Dad and me and the CIA officer who drove us. We had to drive; they wouldn't let us fly. We couldn't even phone ahead to let Uncle Fred and Aunt Jean know we were coming, so they weren't home when we got there. It was a sunny Saturday in August, and they could have been anywhere—though I wondered afterward whether it had been deliberately arranged for them not to be there. I couldn't help but wonder that sort of thing now.

I brought the green dress in its box.

I took it up to my old bedroom in the empty house to change; Uncle Fred and Aunt Jean had never been as particular as Dad about locking doors. I hesitated just for a moment before I slipped off the ribbon, just because it felt so absolutely ridiculous to wear a silk shantung cocktail dress to walk down through the cornfields to the river—and then I pulled the ribbon away and opened the box before I could let myself change my mind.

A Polaroid photograph lay nestled among the tissue papers within.

It was rather out of focus and badly lit, but I recognized myself in my navy pencil dress, and with a bit of squinting I could make out Maksym—just the rough idea of him, really. His face was turned away, and he was mostly swallowed up in the white tablecloth and the shadows along the wall. It was honestly a terrible photo.

There was one line penned on the back in Agent Jones's neat small capitals—P.O. BOX 1210, WASHINGTON D.C.—and a key taped below.

I had been lying for six weeks. They knew me better than I knew myself.

Or, I supposed, they knew Agent Jones.

Our minder waited with the car while Dad and I walked down the little dirt path through the cornfields. The farm backed right up to the river, the Scioto, and there was a little stretch of sandy bank among the Indian grass and young beeches and slabs of river rock. Uncle Fred taught me to fish here. In the mornings and early evenings, you could see white-tailed deer coming down from the woods to drink.

We scattered Mom's ashes there—just Dad and me alone on the riverbank, he in his summer-tan dress uniform and I in that ridiculous cocktail dress. Mom probably would have laughed if she had seen us.

AUTHOR'S NOTE

INDIVIDUAL MIG PILOTS DEFECTED TO the US throughout the Cold War, from all over the Soviet Bloc and for a number of reasons. Two in particular inspired this story.

On March 5, 1953, the day Joseph Stalin died, twenty-one-year-old Polish Air Force Senior Lieutenant Franciszek Jarecki, flying out of the air base at Słupsk near the Baltic coast, suddenly broke formation in his MiG-15 jet fighter and made the minutes-long flight to the Danish island of Bornholm, where he requested political asylum in the West. He eventually made his way to the US, where he was awarded citizenship and fifty thousand dollars—equivalent to more than half a million dollars today. His decision to defect was rooted in his resentment toward the communist regime and in his own family's experience of Soviet oppression during World War II: In 1939, his father, a Polish army officer, was killed by the Soviets during the invasion of Poland.

In September of that same year, 1953, No Kum-Sok of North Korea—also twenty-one, also a senior lieutenant, also piloting a MiG-15—made a daring flight across the 38th parallel to land at a US air base in Seoul. Like Jarecki, No received a cash reward and US citizenship. He learned in 1970, while revisiting Seoul, that his best friend, Lieutenant Kun Soo-Sung, had been executed in reprisal for his defection.

The rest of the story unfolded as I started digging into what happened to Soviet Bloc defectors after they made it to the US. Franciszek Jarecki started a family and founded a business supplying valves to the US Navy; he died in Pennsylvania in 2010. No Kum-Sok likewise started a family; he spent years working in the aeronautical engineering industry and is still alive and living in Florida at the time of this writing. But for many other Soviet defectors—especially those who had worked in Soviet intelligence—the US didn't prove nearly as welcoming.

A 1985 piece in the *Washington Post* ("Case Turns Spotlight on CIA's Handling of Soviet Defectors") reveals some of the hardships defectors faced as they tried to adjust to their new lives in the care of CIA and FBI officials who often "didn't understand who they were, how to handle them, how to meet their needs as human beings"—or who had no interest in doing so. Some defectors became so severely depressed, so unable to cope, that they chose to return home to the Soviet Union despite knowing the punishments that awaited them there. This was the fate of a young Soviet Army defector, Nikolai Ryzhkov, who was sentenced to twelve years in a labor camp upon his return; he and other defectors were profiled in the *New York Times* in a report titled "After They Defect . . ." in 1986.

Sometimes, defectors faced outright abuse and mistreatment at the hands of US intelligence officials. One KGB defector, Yuri Nosenko, was kept in solitary confinement and subjected to harsh interrogation tactics for more than three years in the 1960s. In some cases, this mistreatment stemmed from suspicions that the defections were fake and that the defectors were in fact KGB operatives—and in at least one case, that of Vitaly Yurchenko in the 1980s, this seems to have been true. But in others, US officials neglected or mistreated defectors simply because they viewed them as dishonorable. "They say a guy who defects is a traitor, no matter how you look at it," explains one US intelligence officer in that *New York Times* piece. "And they treat them like dirt."

Rome, New York, and Griffiss Air Force Base are real places, though the base was "realigned" for civilian use in 1993, following the end of the Cold War. Birchwood Park is fictional but modeled closely on the now-demolished Woodhaven Park on Floyd Avenue, which housed Griffiss families for many years until it was abandoned after the realignment of the base. Many of the other places and businesses mentioned—Goldberg's Department Store, the Paul Revere Motor Hotel, the Delta Lake reservoir—were or are important fixtures of the Rome community.

Though there was never a manhunt for a Soviet spy in Rome, to my knowledge, upstate New York *was* the scene of some Cold War espionage intrigue. Alfred Dean Slack—Syracuse native, graduate of the Rochester Institute of Technology, and member of the same spy ring as the Rosenbergs—was held for a while in the Oneida County jail outside Utica following his arrest in Syracuse by agents of the Albany FBI field office in June 1950.

A brief note about Maksym's story: He, like millions of young Ukrainians (along with Poles, Russians, and other Slavs) was an *Ostarbeiter*, a slave laborer for the German Reich during World War II. His experience—including being sent to Auschwitz as punishment for attempting to escape—is drawn from testimonies given by surviving *Ostarbeiter*. (Auschwitz is most infamous for its role in the Holocaust—of the estimated 1.1 million people killed at Auschwitz, around one million were Jews—but non-Jewish prisoners were also sent to Auschwitz throughout the war.) My book *The Silent Unseen* deals with a young Polish *Ostarbeiter*'s experience if you are interested in learning more about these forgotten victims of the Nazi regime.

One thing I learned over the course of researching and writing this story: If I ever started feeling that what I was writing was simply too far-fetched, I could always count on finding some real Cold War spy story that was even more so. For instance, that KGB defector with the poison bullets in his cigarette-case gun was Nikolai Khokhlov; you can read about him in the November 13, 1954, issue of the *Saturday Evening Post*. The KGB tried, unsuccessfully, to assassinate him with poison in 1957. He died in California in 2007 at the age of 85.

ACKNOWLEDGMENTS

I STRUGGLED TO WRITE THIS story against the backdrop of a global pandemic and Russia's genocidal war on Ukraine. I owe an immense debt of gratitude to everybody who helped bring it to publication.

Thanks to Marina Scott, who read and reread multiple drafts and made me keep at it even when I couldn't see a way forward, and to my other early readers—Erin Litteken, Marsha Skrypuch, Adrian Lysenko, Mateusz Świetlicki, Cindy Otis, Marte Mittet, Elizabeth McCrina, Isaiah McCrina, Mary Johnson, and Eva Seyler—for their feedback and encouragement.

Thanks to all the booksellers, educators, librarians, book bloggers and bookstagrammers, fellow writers, and readers whom I've gotten to know over the past few years and whose support has kept me going.

Thanks to production editor Ilana Worrell, copy editor Linda Minton, and proofreader Tracy Koontz; to cover artist Rich Deas; to my designer, Trisha Previte; to my publicist, Morgan Rath; to Katie Quinn and the marketing team; and to everybody at Macmillan Children's, Fierce Reads, and Farrar Straus Giroux Books for Young Readers.

Thanks to my parents, Sharon and David McCrina, for answering any number of random questions about things like military base life or small-town upstate New York in the '50s and '60s.

Thanks to Lieutenant Colonel Howard Zaner and Colonel Robert Goering, US Air Force (retired), for so generously sharing with me the details of their time at Griffiss Air Force Base and the Rome Air Development Center. Any inaccuracies and liberties taken are my own.

Thanks to my agent, Jennie Kendrick, for her voice of reason and her enthusiasm for this project.

And, finally, to my long-suffering editor, Wes Adams—it's an honor to work with you. Thank you.